"I don't want yo
shoulders shrug
backward toward her camper. "I don't
even know who you are. Just, please,
forget you ever found me."

No, she wasn't running away from him. Not now, not after Mack had tried so hard and fought so long to find her.

A black and windowless van flew around the corner at a speed that shocked him. A huge man in dark fatigues sat in the front seat. The snarling face of some kind of wild animal with large jagged teeth was painted on the front of his camo-green mask. It was a Jackal, and one with the very same build and mask as the one who'd shot him outside Iris's apartment and left him for dead.

"Iris!" Mack shouted. "Run!"

The Jackal leaned out the window and fired.

Mack leaped, pushing Iris out of the way just as he felt the sharp sting of a tranquilizer dart pierce his neck.

Maggie K. Black is an award-winning journalist and romantic suspense author with an insatiable love of traveling the world. She has lived in the American South, Europe and the Middle East. She now makes her home in Canada with her history-teacher husband, their two beautiful girls and a small but mighty dog. Maggie enjoys connecting with her readers at maggiekblack.com.

Books by Maggie K. Black

Love Inspired Suspense

Protected Identities

Christmas Witness Protection
Runaway Witness

True North Heroes

Undercover Holiday Fiancée
The Littlest Target
Rescuing His Secret Child
Cold Case Secrets

Amish Witness Protection

Amish Hideout

Military K-9 Unit

Standing Fast

True North Bodyguards

Kidnapped at Christmas
Rescue at Cedar Lake
Protective Measures

Visit the Author Profile page at Harlequin.com for more titles.

RUNAWAY WITNESS

MAGGIE K. BLACK

LOVE INSPIRED SUSPENSE
INSPIRATIONAL ROMANCE

LOVE INSPIRED® SUSPENSE

INSPIRATIONAL ROMANCE

ISBN-13: 978-1-335-40262-2

Recycling programs
for this product may
not exist in your area.

Runaway Witness

This is a work of fiction. Names, characters, places and incidents are either the
product of the author's imagination or are used fictitiously. Any resemblance
to actual persons, living or dead, businesses, companies, events or locales is
entirely coincidental.

This edition published by arrangement with Harlequin Books S.A.

For questions and comments about the quality of this book,
please contact us at CustomerService@Harlequin.com.

Love Inspired
22 Adelaide St. West, 40th Floor
Toronto, Ontario M5H 4E3, Canada
www.Harlequin.com

Printed in U.S.A.

What man of you, having an hundred sheep, if he lose one of them, doth not leave the ninety and nine in the wilderness, and go after that which is lost, until he find it? And when he hath found it, he layeth it on his shoulders, rejoicing. Either what woman having ten pieces of silver, if she lose one piece, doth not light a candle, and sweep the house, and seek diligently till she find it? And when she hath found it, she calleth her friends and her neighbours together, saying, Rejoice with me; for I have found the piece which I had lost.

–Luke 15:4-5, 8-9

This book is dedicated to the woman who was working at a truck stop in Georgia at three in the morning, years ago, when I was on a road trip. She told me to go ahead and sleep in my car overnight in front of her window, because she'd pray and sing to the Lord for me while I was sleeping, watch over me, and make sure I was safe.

I think about her faith and kindness a lot.

ONE

Iris James's hands shook as she piled dirty dishes high on her tray. Something about the look of the bearded man in the corner booth was unsettlingly familiar. He'd been nursing his coffee way longer than anyone had any business loitering around a highway diner in the middle of nowhere, in the northern regions of Ontario, even if there was a snowstorm brewing outside. But it wasn't until she noticed the telltale lump of a gun hidden underneath his red plaid jacket that she realized he might be there to kill her.

She shifted the tray of dirty dishes into the crook of her arm and slid her hand deep into the pocket of her waitress's uniform, feeling for the small handgun tucked behind her order pad.

Then she glanced around the crowded diner and prayed.

If today's the day Oscar Underwood's hit men finally catch me, please get someone to find and rescue every last person he kidnapped. And don't let anyone in this diner right now get hurt in the crossfire.

It was six thirty at night, the late-February sun would be setting soon and the dinner rush was in full swing. Iris stepped behind an empty table and watched the man out of the corner of her eye as she quickly added more dishes to her growing pile.

Growing up poor in a small Canadian town, she'd first gotten a gun to protect herself against wild animals, never imagining she'd ever need it for protection against kidnappers or killers. But then she'd become a social worker, opened a homeless drop-in center in Toronto and started hearing rumors that Underwood's men had been kidnapping strong and healthy street youth and homeless people in their late teens and early twenties to work on his remote farms and ranches.

The homeless said Underwood used a team of masked "Jackals" to subdue and tranquilize their victims. Police had called it a ridiculous urban legend. Iris had done everything she could to get the authorities to take action, including camping outside the Toronto mayor's office.

But no one listened. Not until the kindest, sweetest and most understanding man she'd ever known— a homeless center volunteer named Mack Gray—had been murdered.

She'd agreed to testify at Underwood's trial and go into witness protection until then. But criminal hackers had stolen her witness protection file and sold it to Underwood. She'd dropped out of witness protection's care, disappeared from the new life they'd given her and had been on the run from the Jackals ever since, dyeing her blond hair various shades of brown, living out of a camper trailer and never stopping anywhere for more than a few days at a time.

Iris dropped her tray of dirty dishes on the counter and grabbed a steaming pot of coffee, pulling it off the percolator so quickly it splashed and sizzled on the heating element. She wove through the tables, praying for wisdom, topping up mugs and watching him out of the corner of her eye. The man was taller than his slouch implied, with a thick black beard and a Montreal Canadiens baseball cap shoved down so low she could barely see his face. But even as he seemed to avert his gaze when she glanced his direction, she couldn't shake the feeling he'd been watching her.

And that she'd definitely seen him somewhere before. Something about the line of his jaw unsettled her in a way she couldn't begin to understand.

A shiver ran down her spine and she gripped the coffeepot tighter to keep it from shaking. As if sensing her eyes on him, the bearded man glanced up, and for a fraction of a second she caught sight of a pair of piercing blue eyes before his gaze dropped back to his coffee.

Mack?

Hot tears filled her vision and her hands began to shake so hard that the coffee sloshed in the pot she carried. *No! It can't be! Come on, Iris, get a grip on yourself.*

Mack's body had been found floating in Lake Ontario eight weeks ago with two bullets in his back. This man was at least ten pounds lighter than Mack, with a nose that was much wider and a chin a lot squarer than Mack's had been.

"Hey, waitress!" A large trucker from the group at the table by the window snatched hold of her wrist as she passed and jerked her back a step. "Don't be so stingy. Leave the pot."

She yanked her hand away, scalding coffee sloshing over her arm as she did so. A chorus of crude laughter rose from the table of truckers in front of her.

"Pay your bill and get out!" The diner's gray-haired owner, Colleen, clapped sharply at the men as if they were wayward chickens and stormed across the room. "Nobody touches my staff. And leave a decent tip behind you!"

The diminutive woman stood by the table with her arms crossed as the men each dropped a twenty on the table, grabbed the remains of their sandwiches and skedaddled into the snow without waiting for change.

Colleen glanced at Iris. Soft lines crinkled her face. "You all right?"

Iris nodded. When she'd packed everything she owned into the tiny camper, emptying her bank account and going on the run, she'd managed to take with her a large laminated map of the country, on which she'd marked all the locations that street youth had told her they'd been able to go off the grid for help, food, safety and work. What had once been a passion project to help her better understand the lives of those who came through the center's doors had now become a roadmap to her own survival.

She'd visited close to a hundred so far as she'd crisscrossed the country. They hadn't all panned out. A few she'd suspected had been fronts for criminal activity and for some others she'd barely arrived before the still-small voice inside her told her it was time to leave. But most had been filled with kind and compassionate strangers, like Colleen, and guilt welled up inside Iris, knowing she was about to disappear on her before her shift was done. She glanced back at the bearded man in the booth.

He was gone.

Iris's heartbeat quickened as her eyes darted around the room. He was nowhere to be seen. At least while she could watch him, she'd felt like she had some control over the situation. Now he was out there, somewhere, like an animal waiting to strike.

"You'll be surprised to see just how many people who come in here would rather drop a twenty than bother to do math," Colleen said, dragging Iris's attention back to the table. In their hurry to leave, the men had left a hundred dollars on a forty-one-dollar bill. Colleen swept up the pile of twenties and handed them to Iris. "Cash out the bill and consider whatever's leftover your tip. I'm just sorry you had to put up with that."

"Thank you." Iris swallowed hard, scooped the dirty dishes onto a tray and picked it up. If she'd been able to wait out just three more days, she would have gotten over six hundred dollars in her first paycheck. But every inch of nerves running down her spine told her not to wait another minute. "I really hate asking this, but I wondered if I could get a small cash advance on my pay for food and gas?"

She held her breath, but Colleen didn't even blink. "There are two one-hundred-dollar bills underneath the tray in the cash register. Take them and make a note in the ledger. You all right?"

"I will be," Iris said. "Thank you."

Iris turned quickly and hurried to the counter before Colleen could see the guilt and fear filling her eyes. She dropped off the dishes, cashed out the bill, took the two hundreds and her tip and headed through the kitchen, grabbing her jacket off a hook. She pushed through the back door and scanned her surroundings. Not a person in sight. Winter air stung her skin. Snow swirled down around her and the gray February sky spread above her, hemmed in by dark green conifers.

She zipped herself into her jacket and pulled the hood down tight as she ran for the tree line and then through the snow-covered woods until she reached the abandoned gas station where she'd parked her big black truck. She'd paid cash for the small secondhand camper trailer attached to the hitch and that had been her home for the past few weeks.

Almost there. All she had to do was make it across the parking lot, get to her camper, leap inside and hit the road.

The bearded man stepped out from behind the gas station.

She stopped short, yanked the small handgun from her pocket and pointed it at him with both hands. "Whoever you are, get down! Now!"

"Don't shoot!" His hands rose. "It's me! Mack!"

Her heart froze. The shape of his face was slightly wrong, and seeing him here and now defied all logic. Yet somehow she knew that voice with every beat of her heart.

The gun shook in her hands. "I told you to get down!"

"Iris! I'm an undercover cop!"

Detective Mack Gray's heart pounded so hard as he stared into Iris's hazel eyes that the bullet wounds left by a Jackal ached in his chest. How was she even more tenacious and more beautiful than he remembered?

He'd gone undercover with the Royal Canadian Mounted Police to investigate claims that Oscar Underwood was kidnapping street people to work at his remote farms and ranches. For some unexplained reason, local Toronto police were turning a blind eye to it. Mack had volunteered at the homeless drop-in center in order to protect Oscar's latest target—the head social worker. And he'd completely underestimated just what a force of nature she would turn out to be.

Iris James had this huge heart that made street youth open up to her, combined with a sheer tenacity that kept her hounding the mayor's office and harping at local police no matter how much they dismissed her. When he'd been shot and nearly killed by one of Underwood's Jackals, Mack had thought he'd never see her again.

Now, despite the handgun clutched in her hands, it took all his self-control not to try to hug her.

"I'm part of what I guess you could call an off-the-grid witness protection task force. Helping those whose secret identity files were stolen and sold in the recent data hack at Christmas," Mack said. "I've been looking for you for weeks. I know I look a bit different, but that's only because I'm wearing facial prosthetics. The nephew of one of our guys is a whiz when it comes to creating disguises—"

"Mack Gray is dead." The words left her mouth like the crack of a whip.

He felt his jaw drop. Dead? Whichever cop had come up with that cover for his disappearance had left it out of the files.

"I was injured," he said, keeping his hands raised, "but I survived."

"Mack Gray was shot." Iris punctuated her words by jabbing at the air with the gun like it was a teacher's chalkboard pointer. "Twice. Then tossed into Lake Ontario by one of Underwood's Jackals."

Well, that part was true at least.

"I was hit with a tranquilizer dart first," he admitted, "then shot twice with a handgun and then they tried to drown me."

The memory reared up suddenly and painfully inside his mind. It had been just him and Iris alone in the homeless center that night, cleaning up and talking long after it had closed.

She'd been upset about the missing street youth, he'd walked her home to her tiny ground-floor apartment in one of the less desirable parts of the city, and despite the fact he was supposed to keep a professional distance from his targets, he'd found himself wrapping his arms around her. He'd held her tightly and promised her that no matter what it took, Underwood would be stopped and all the people he'd forced into working for him would be found.

She'd gone inside, but he'd stayed there, asking God to help him handle whatever the strange and overwhelming emotions he felt for her were that seemed to be cascading inside him.

That's when he'd seen the man, clad in dark fatigues, with a horrific snarling face painted on his camo-green ski mask. With a tranquilizer gun in his hand, he'd tried to open Iris's window.

And Mack had seen red.

Despite not having permission to engage or break cover unless Iris's life was in imminent danger, Mack had chased him off. He'd pursued the man through Toronto's back alleys until there'd been a flash, then a bang of a gun, and then all was a blur of pain. He'd woken up in the hospital three days later, with holes in his chest, machines keeping him alive and a buddy breaking the news he was on probation pending internal investigation.

"I'm sorry," he said. "I didn't realize you thought I was dead. I should've tried to find out what cover story they'd given you. Usually they go with something far less dramatic, like a sick grandmother in Moosonee." He considered telling her about the Jackal outside her window and then decided what mattered most was calming her down. That was one thing he'd always been good at. "But yeah, I was shot by a Jackal in an ugly camouflage green animal mask. It was touch and go for a long time and doctors thought I wasn't going to make it. If it helps, I was actually legally dead for a moment."

He tried to grin as he added the last part in a feeble attempt to lighten the mood.

"Are you seriously trying to joke about almost dying?" Iris demanded.

"Yeah," he admitted. "Though judging by the look on your face, that wasn't the right call." He resisted the urge to point out she'd always seemed to find his lame jokes funny before. "I'm sorry, I'm really cold right now and I didn't exactly plan out what I was going to say when I found you."

Fire flashed in her eyes. "And now that you've found me, what do you want?"

Your forgiveness. The words crossed his mind and surprised him.

"I want you to go back into witness protection until Underwood's trial," he said. "I know we let you down last time. But the Jackals won't stop looking for you until you're dead and as your friend—"

"You are not my friend," she cut him off. "I don't even know who you are anymore. Because the Mack Gray I knew would never lie to me! He was the only person on my side fighting to stop Underwood and would never use me or pretend to care about me, as part of some undercover ruse!"

He opened his mouth to try to explain himself but the pain in his chest tightened so sharply he could barely breathe.

"Iris." He started toward her. Instinctively his arms

parted to pull her into his chest. "I'm really, really sorry—"

"Stop." She raised her free hand like a traffic cop. "You don't get to hug me. Not now. Not ever again. I lost one of the best friends I've ever had in my life. Twice. First when a cop showed up at my door and told me Mack Gray was dead, and again right now when you told me our whole relationship was fake and our friendship didn't exist to begin with. I want you to go, leave me alone and forget that you ever found me."

A black, windowless van flew around the corner at a speed that shocked him. A huge man in dark fatigues sat in the front seat. The snarling face of some kind of wild animal with large jagged teeth was painted on the front of his camo-green mask. It was a Jackal, with the very same mask as the one who'd shot him outside Iris's apartment and left him for dead.

"Iris!" Mack shouted. "Run!"

The Jackal leaned out the window and fired.

Mack pushed Iris out of the way just as he felt the sharp sting of a tranquilizer dart pierce his neck.

TWO

Iris's feet pelted across the expansive parking lot and toward the safety of the truck. Behind her she could hear the Jackal's van coming and Mack shouting at her to run. Panic welled up inside her throat. Somehow, one of Underwood's Jackals had finally found her and for the first time in her life she saw with her own eyes the terrifying painted face mask she'd only heard whispered rumors of.

Gunfire filled the air, then came a deafening bang and a screech of metal, and she glanced back. Mack had shot one of the tires out, sending the van flying into a pole.

"Go on without me!" Mack called behind her. "Don't stop! I'll find you!"

How? She didn't even know how he'd found her the first time. The Mack she'd gotten to know over the four months he'd volunteered at the center had claimed to be a recently laid-off dishwasher. He'd been gentle, sweet and the last man she'd have ever pegged for a cop. The first time they'd met had been when he'd come to her aid when the mayor's chief of security had been roughly trying to force her out of City Hall. At the time, Mack had just calmly stepped in between them, like some kind of peacemaker, and in cool, measured tones, told the other man to back off and let go of her.

But now, as the van door opened and the green-masked Jackal leaped out, Mack ran right at him, like a football player going in for the tackle.

Her heartbeat thudded. A tranquilizer dart hung loose from Mack's neck, seemingly tangled in his scarf. He'd been shot! The heavy sedative would be streaming through his veins, slowing his movements until unconsciousness swept over him and he passed out.

Despite every conflicted feeling swirling inside her, the sight of Mack in danger stabbed like a knife to her heart. She might not like what he'd done or the fact he'd somehow found her, but she couldn't bear the thought of watching him die in front of her now.

The Jackal raised the tranq gun and fired at Mack again. She held her breath and prayed. *Help him, Lord!* One tranquilizer dart could put him to sleep for hours. Two might kill him.

She watched, almost frozen in place, as Mack dropped to the ground and rolled. The second dart flew past him and went skimming across the snowy ground. Then Mack spun back and threw himself at the masked man, grabbing the dart gun with both hands and wrestling it from his grasp.

The Jackal swung hard, leveling Mack with a swift blow. The Jackal reached for the holster at his side, but Mack didn't give him the opportunity to grab his handgun. The detective reared up and swung back, striking the Jackal with a strong blow of his own.

"Iris!" Mack shouted, his voice ragged as he panted for breath. "Go! Get out of here! I'll hold him off!"

All she had to do was get in her truck, gun the engine and hit the open road. She'd managed to hide from Underwood and his Jackals for this long. She'd evade them again.

But how could she just take off and leave Mack fighting for his life? Whoever he was and whatever he'd done, he deserved better than that. She'd lost him once. She wouldn't lose him again.

At least, not like this.

She braced her feet on the ground and pulled her weapon. "Stop! Or I'll fire! And I'm not shooting darts!"

But when she tried to set the Jackal in her sights, she realized it was no use. She couldn't get a clear shot. If she fired, she could hit Mack. All she could do was watch helplessly as the masked man tried to beat Mack down, while he deflected blow after blow. He fought back with a strength, skill and ferocity that she had never imagined the gentle man she'd known could possess.

Who are you, Mack Gray? Why did you come looking for me?

All he had to do was break free long enough to make a run for it, leap into the truck and let her drive them to safety. But she could see Mack was flagging.

Then it happened, the Jackal caught him with a single, hard left hook to the temple that sent Mack flying.

A cry slipped from her lips as she watched him hit the ground and roll.

Get up! Come on, get up!

The Jackal turned and ran toward her. Mack hauled himself up to his feet and jumped on the Jackal's back, clutching a tranquilizer dart in his hand. He jabbed it hard into the Jackal's shoulder. With a roar, the masked man tossed him off onto the ground. This time, Mack didn't get up.

"I need backup!" the Jackal shouted into the walkie-talkie at his lapel as he charged across the lot toward her. "Hurry! I've been hit with a tranquilizer!"

For one brief fraction of a second, she glanced past him to where Mack now lay limp on his stomach on the ground. She prayed for him to move. His head raised, and his piercing blue eyes met hers in a glance.

"Go…" The word moved silently on Mack's lips. "Run."

Iris threw herself into the driver's seat, slammed the door behind her and slid the key into the ignition. The Jackal hesitated, like he didn't know whether to finish Mack or go for Iris. She didn't give him the choice. She turned the key, hit the gas and the truck shot across the parking lot toward them.

The green-masked Jackal raised his handgun toward her and fired.

Fatigue crashed over Mack, like a heavy wave pressing his body into the cold, wet ground. At the corner of his consciousness, he was barely aware of a vehicle roaring closer and gunshots firing, but it was like it

was happening to someone else and very far away. He'd
seen the effects of tranquilizers on other people firsthand and he knew he'd had it in his system when he'd
been found shot in Lake Ontario. But now he actually
felt it, a weird numbing and tingling feeling, heavier
than any sedative he'd ever experienced. It coursed
through his system and threatened to drag him under.

Desperate prayers filled his core. Frustration surged
through him. His palms pushed futilely against the
ground as he tried to get to his feet, but his body would
barely move. He couldn't die like this, not here and not
now. He'd almost died once before and had woken up to
find his career in jeopardy and Iris gone. The months
he'd spent undercover volunteering at the center had
been the happiest of his life and Iris had been the reason why. He'd just found her again and couldn't lose
his life in front of her now.

*Lord, please don't let Iris get hurt because of me.
Please stop the Jackals for good and make sure every
young person they kidnapped for Underwood is found.*
He tried to open his eyes, but it was like an invisible
force was pressing his eyelids down. *And have mercy
on me, Lord, if this is it. I don't know how I'm going
to get out of this one alive.*

The ground shook with the vibrations of a vehicle
coming toward him. The rumble of the motor grew
louder, he felt wind rush past him, and then tires
screeched so close to his head he thought for a moment they were going to drive over him. He heard a
vehicle door open and a voice calling to him, breaking through the haze.

"Mack!" Iris shouted. Her footsteps pounded toward him. "Come on, Mack, get up!"

I would if I could.

He forced his eyes open. The side of Iris's brown-and-white camper was less than three feet away from his head. Then he saw Iris, sprinting across the ground and dropping beside him like a runner stealing home base.

"Get up! Now!" Her voice, sharp and strong, filled his ears.

"I..." He pushed his words sluggishly over his lips. "I can't..."

"Yes, you can," she said. "You've seen what this sedative does to people. You've helped me get them out of gutters, through the door and onto the couch, or into your car to drive to the hospital. And I've seen how tough you are firsthand."

She shoved her shoulder under his arm and hauled him up. He stumbled to his feet.

"Now come on. You did a great job stabbing the Jackal with that dart. He's run back to his van. Probably started feeling the effects and doesn't want to pass out on the ground. But he called for backup, and I really don't want to be here when more Jackals arrive."

Iris was a force of nature. He'd never known anyone or anything that could stand up to her. He'd seen her forcibly remove disruptive people from the center's free community meals and help scoop vulnerable youth up off the sidewalk on cold nights and bring them inside to warm up while she found an overnight shelter to take them. And now here she was, half dragging and half helping him across the pavement as he leaned against her.

"I...heard...gunshots..."

"Yup." She reached the camper and yanked the door open. "He fired at me and missed, probably because of the sedative dart you stuck him with. Which is awesome and thanks again for that, because I really like my truck."

Mack almost chuckled. Humor in the face of danger was a good quality to have. So was tenacity.

She hauled him through the doorway into the camper and he stumbled in. It was small, with a bunk-size bed set high into the wall on one side. Underneath it was a small table and a cushioned bench. A counter with shelves was adjacent under a large window. A laminated map of Canada covered almost all of the opposite wall, scrawled with words, squiggles and lines. It was the map from her apartment, showing the routes the homeless had taken across Canada. Photographs of some of the street youth who'd come to the homeless center were taped around the corners. He noticed she'd circled the faces of all those they suspected the Jackals had kidnapped but who hadn't been found in the raids of Underwood's farms and complexes.

"Are you looking for them?" he asked, mumbling the words.

"Well, I haven't given up on them."

His legs bumped against the bench. She gently pushed him to lie down, checking his eyes and his pulse as she did do.

"Sorry to bring you in here and not the truck," she

said, "but my truck's a lot higher off the ground and I don't think I can lift you all the way up to get you into the passenger seat. So, you're going to sleep it off in here and I'm going to get us out of here."

But his vehicle was parked not ten minutes away, complete with equipment, supplies, weapons and disguises. Plus, he desperately needed to coordinate with his team.

He heard the sound of another vehicle approaching. Iris's eyes scanned the map.

"Just sleep and trust me," she said. "I'll get us to the closest safe place I can and we can regroup from there."

No, that wasn't the plan. He was here to talk her into letting witness protection safeguard her, not go on the run with her.

She jumped out and shut the door behind her, leaving him alone in the camper. There was the sound of fresh gunfire and voices shouting.

No, it wasn't going to go down like this.

He pushed himself up off the bench and stumbled for the door. He wasn't going to stay in here while she was out there in danger. He heard the truck's engine roar and then the trailer lurched, yanking the door from his hand, even as he turned the handle. The door swung open in front of him and he fell toward it, barely grabbing the doorframe to keep from falling through as trees rushed past him. Bullets ricocheted against the side of the camper.

He had to help Iris.

Then the camper swerved wildly, he fell back hard against the bench, the door slammed shut and unconsciousness swept over him.

THREE

So far she'd been either savvy enough or blessed enough not to run into any of Underwood's Jackals. She gripped the steering wheel and allowed herself one quick glance in her side mirror at the van following her. Now she'd left a green-masked Jackal behind in an empty parking lot and had a red-masked one on her tail on an empty Canadian highway. Her truck was probably strong enough to outrun them, but not with the camper attached to the back. Not to mention, a sedated Mack inside.

Her heart stuttered. How had Mack even found her? Why would a man who'd built his entire relationship with her on a false identity and a fake story cross the country and search so long and hard just to talk her into going back into witness protection? She cast another glance at the van behind her. Her chin rose, and she gunned the engine, pushing the truck faster and faster. Her eyes cut to the rearview mirror and the camper behind her. She whispered a prayer under her breath.

Help me, God. Please keep Mack safe.

Then she yanked the steering wheel hard to her right, in a U-turn. The truck spun, and its tires squealed as they slid on the hard-packed snow. She felt the pull of the camper as it spun out behind her, threatening to pull them off the road, and she prayed the trailer hitch wouldn't break.

The red-masked Jackal was speeding toward her now, head-on, in a game of chicken down the empty highway. She waited, second after second, as he grew closer. Did he think she'd swerve? If so, he didn't know who he was dealing with.

With her left hand, she slipped the gun from her pocket and rolled the window down. The Jackal drew closer, until she could see every line of the snarling animal painted on his mask. He raised his weapon.

She fired first. A single bullet flew from her gun, and his windshield shattered. The van spun off the road and into the snow-filled ditch as she sped by. She held her breath and watched the crashed vehicle in the side mirror until she saw the Jackal stumble from the wreckage. She breathed a prayer of thanksgiving that he'd survived the crash and that she hadn't killed him.

She fixed her eyes on the road ahead and drove. Within moments, the few remaining scattered buildings of the town had disappeared into the side mirror, leaving nothing but endless tall pine trees and sky spreading ahead.

She started looking for a gap in the woods, until finally she spotted a thin and narrow dirt road jutting out of the trees to her right. She scanned the highway for any sign of a vehicle, and seeing none, she pulled off, weaving down the winding path between dense trees until the highway itself disappeared in the distance.

Only then did she cut the engine, climb out and run back to the trailer. She yanked the door open. Dishes, books and clothing lay scattered across the floor. There in the middle lay Mack. He'd apparently come to long enough to wrap himself up tightly in a warm and heavy wool blanket that she guessed had fallen from her bunk. He snored gently.

"Mack?" She knelt down beside him.

He nodded as if hearing her and smiled slightly, but his eyes stayed closed. His ridiculous facial prosthetic had slipped, making it look like his nose was on an angle. She ran her fingers along the lines of his face, feeling the disguise give slightly under her fingertips. Slowly she pulled the prosthetic off, peeling back the rubbery substance to feel the soft authentic skin of the sweetest, kindest and then ultimately the most upsettingly confusing man she'd ever met underneath.

"Your pulse is still good," she said. "Your skin isn't clammy and the fact you're snoring is a good thing. You probably just need to sleep, but I don't know if we want to risk it. I'm over an hour from the closest hospital, but I'll take you there and drop you off at the emergency room."

"No, no, don't." Mack shook his head. His eyes fluttered open. "I'm okay. Just sleepy."

She sat back on her heels. "Are you sure?"

"We stay together," he said, and his words came out so slowly she had to fight the urge to interrupt. "You and me. No splitting up. And I only go to public

hospitals in an emergency, just in case someone rec-
ognizes me and it blows a case."

She wasn't sure if she should be taking directions
from someone who was barely awake. Or what she
thought of him living a life that kept him from getting
help if he needed it. Then again, she didn't have any
idea what risks she'd be putting Mack or herself in if
she pulled up to a random hospital. If this dart affected
him the same as the other ones she'd seen, he'd sleep
it off and be back to his normal self soon, and there
were definite benefits to staying hidden as long as the
Jackals were so close on their tail.

"Okay, well, I'm still going to drive in that general
direction," she said, "and I'll stop and check in with
you every fifteen to twenty minutes. If I see any warning signs or you get worse, I'm speeding there."

His eyes closed again, as if somehow that satisfied
him. "Okay, and my team will help."

Only his team wasn't here, and she had no idea how
to contact them.

"Don't worry," she said. "I'll keep you safe."

"I know," he said, "you're Iris." He rolled over and,
in a moment, resumed snoring.

She stood slowly. Had she really just promised
to take care of this man after everything he'd done?
Somehow it felt so natural to talk to him like one of the
people at her homeless center back in Toronto. Even if
she now didn't know if any of his stories about growing up in struggle and poverty, like she had, were real.

Her heart ached, wondering how the acting man-
ager and volunteers at the center were coping without

her at the helm. She prayed for the day all this would be over and she'd be able to go back to her normal life. She started tidying up the camper. She'd leave worrying about what to do for Mack for last.

"Why did you go to the trouble of becoming my friend?" she asked him. "You know me. I would've told anyone who listened what the street youth were saying about Underwood and the Jackals. You could've shown up at my door dressed like a cop, flashed your badge and I'd have told you everything. Instead, you wormed your way into my life. We spent hours together every day, working at the center, praying together, going out for food and telling stories about our lives—stories that I don't even know are true anymore. You became the best friend I ever had. Why would you do that to me?"

But Mack snored gently and didn't answer.

Mack slept fitfully, barely able to open his eyes for more than moments at a time before the pressing fatigue swept over him again. Iris's reassuring voice floated in and out at the edges of his mind. Soft warmth surrounded him now; Iris had somehow pulled the mattress of her bunk onto the floor and helped him roll onto it before sticking a pillow under his head and practically burying him in blankets. He was vaguely aware of the vehicle moving for a while and then stopping again. Iris popped in to offer him water, reminded him to stay hydrated and chatted to him briefly before leaving again and going back to driving.

She'd definitely been attentive, but in a way that wasn't over-the-top. Instead, he just felt safe and also guilty that the woman he'd hurt and come looking for was now taking care of him.

There'd been no more Jackal sightings, from what he'd heard of Iris's 911 call. She'd kept her description of the attempted abduction anonymous and vague. He'd barely been able to sit up, let alone contact his team. There were probably at least two Jackals on the loose, one of whom he was fairly certain was the same man who'd tried to break into Iris's apartment two months ago.

The fact Iris had brought her map of the country with her certainly explained how she'd managed to stay hidden for so long and how she'd managed to stay off the grid. It was also a testimony to the close and trusting relationships she'd developed with people at the homeless center over the years. It was smart and he was impressed, but it was nothing compared to the life and safety he and his team would be able to provide Iris when she went back into witness protection.

Not that he'd done a very good job of convincing her so far. But he'd spent his life moving in the shadows, pretending to be the kind of man he wasn't and convincing the worst of thugs to turn against their bosses and criminals to trust him with their secrets. How difficult could it be to convince a spunky, kindhearted, talkative social worker to go back into witness protection?

The camper stopped again. His eyes opened and he sat up, his head finally feeling clear. Darkness filled the windows. A battery-operated alarm clock told him it was just past nine o'clock at night, and a soft buffeting sound against the windows told him the snow had started again.

The door swung open, bringing a fresh blast of February air with it. A light shone briefly in his eyes, before the beam dropped to the floor at Iris's feet.

"Mack," she said softly. "You're up."

"Pretty much," he said. "How long was I out?"

"Almost two hours," she said.

He blinked as the time on the clock finally sank in. His team hadn't heard from him since he'd run out of the diner to follow Iris. He was now a two-hour drive from his truck and its small cache of weapons, disguises, food rations, all the best electronic gadgets an undercover detective could need and a bag of essentials for Iris for when he found her. He ran his hand over his head, vaguely aware that she'd pulled the itchy prosthetics off his face. The glue that had been holding them on remained like scar tissue.

Lord, I'm really thankful that she managed to get us out of there alive. If it hadn't been for her quick thinking, we could both be dead right now. But please help me get this mission back on track pronto.

Iris set the flashlight on the counter, directing it toward him like a spotlight, locked the door and knelt beside him. At some point since escaping the diner, she'd yanked a pair of jeans on underneath the skirt of her waitress uniform, and the soft flashlight glow sent golden highlights dancing along the maple brown hair that fell in loose waves around her shoulders. His breath caught. How was she even more beautiful than he'd remembered?

"How are you feeling?" she asked.

"Thirsty and a bit sore, but good, everything considered," Mack said. "Thank you so much for getting us out of there alive and managing to hide well enough that the Jackals apparently haven't tracked us." He rolled his head from one side to the other, cracking his neck. "Where are we now?"

"Outside some kind of a farming complex." She frowned. "The map is a bit hit-and-miss. I'd gotten the impression from the kids who told me about it that Crow's Farm was the kind of place they could camp at while they pitched in a few days to make some honest cash. Some of them were talking about it as a safe alternative to working at one of Underwood's places." She shrugged. "But I built this map on rumors and gossip, not facts. Sometimes it lets me down, and this is one of those times. Crow's Farm isn't a farm. It's basically a big walled complex with some greenhouse-type buildings inside. But there's a pretty big campground less than an hour from here we can try next."

Mack grabbed both of her hands in his, feeling the familiar softness of her fingertips. "Or you can stop running and risking your life," he said. "Let my team bring you in and go back into witness protection."

She sat back on her heels and pulled her hands away. "Because the police were such great listeners when I was trying to get someone to believe that Oscar Underwood was abducting people and forcing them to work at his farms?" she asked. "Or because witness protection did such a great job of protecting me?"

Okay, maybe he should've been prepared for this.

Iris had always been headstrong and both local and federal police had let her down in different ways. But what she didn't know was the incredible work his team had done since the witness protection files were breached and how they'd quickly found new lives for people whose identities had been auctioned off.

He ran his hand over his face. "You don't have a lot of faith in the cops."

"I have absolutely no faith in the cops." She crossed her arms. "Police brushed me off, time and time again, and did nothing to help protect young people from Underwood and his Jackals."

"That's not true." Mack grabbed the counter and stood, feeling his back straighten and shoulders broaden as he did so. "At least one cop took you very seriously. Me. The RCMP was well aware that local police, for whatever reason, weren't taking the claims against Underwood seriously. So, I went undercover to find out if there was any truth to the rumors. I'm really sorry the local cops were dismissive of you—of us—all those times I went and filed reports with you." He scowled. "Believe me, as a detective, it really got under my skin to see you brushed off like that. But at the same time, you also have to realize just how kooky you sounded when you claimed men in ski masks with animal faces painted on were abducting homeless youth. Not to mention how often people like the kind you care for in your homeless center lie to police. Those in authority were right to be skeptical. None of those missing kids even gave you their real names. Or called you by yours, for that matter. When you asked them to call you either 'Iris' or 'Miss James,' they called you 'Missy.'"

"Now you sound just like a cop." She pushed herself to her feet. "And somehow now you look like a cop, too. The Mack I knew had this way of standing that made me feel relaxed and safe. He never stood with his chest all puffed out like that."

Well, she'd never challenged his authority before. Or prevented him from trying to save her.

"If I look like a cop, it's because I am one," he said. "I'm an RCMP detective and have been in law enforcement for a decade. And in case you missed it, I just said local police were wrong to dismiss you the way they did, even if they were right to be skeptical. I'd still really like to know if it was just inherent bias against the homeless or if something more nefarious was going on. Oscar Underwood and his henchmen got away with too much for too long unchecked. But the RCMP had a whole investigation into Oscar Underwood, and your assistance was vital in that."

"My assistance?" She shot the words back at him. "You pretended to be my friend."

"I *was* your friend!" His voice filled the camper.

"I thought you were dead!" Her voice matched his. "Do you know what it's like to think someone you care about has been murdered?"

Yeah, he did. Although in his case, they had actually died and stayed dead. He'd lost a couple of fellow officers and a more than a few informants in his work with the RCMP, which was why he never let himself get close to anyone he met undercover. Well, until Iris somehow burrowed her way under his defenses. He swallowed a breath and forced his voice to lower.

"I'm unbelievably sorry about that," he said. "And I would've contacted you the moment I was out of intensive care, only by then you were already in witness protection and I wasn't allowed to contact you or know anything about where you were placed. Then when I heard your file was compromised and you'd disappeared off the grid, I was worried sick. I know there's nothing I can say to make up for how I hurt you," he went on. "But while I didn't tell you some things as part of my investigation, I never lied to you about who I was as a person or the man I am inside. You have no idea how hard I worked to find you and make sure you were safe."

"How did you even find me?" she asked.

"It wasn't easy," he admitted. "When the files were stolen and auctioned off online, a few RCMP officers and a hacker came together as a secret task force to take the criminals down. I'd only been out of the hospital a few weeks and was still not allowed to return to regular work." *Suspended.* That was the word he should say but somehow couldn't get past his lips. "Two of my colleagues stopped the auction, but not before eighteen identities were sold. We then focused our attention on helping those whose identities had been compromised. Most were easy to track down and relocate into new lives. Others, like you, were a lot harder to find."

Something hardened in her eyes. "That didn't answer my question."

Yeah, she'd never been one for accepting vague answers. Or giving up easily.

"I called in every favor I could think of," he admitted. "Specifically I talked to a lot of criminals. I've been an undercover detective for a very long time and have met hundreds of unsavory people. My colleague Liam took the other side of the coin and talked to a lot of cops. A lot of people in law enforcement owe him a favor. Our hacker, Seth, ran online searches. When we'd gathered enough data points, I got in my truck and drove and started tracking you in the good old-fashioned, boots-on-the-ground way."

He hadn't slept in days and hadn't stopped thinking of her once since the moment they'd last said goodbye.

"And why?" Iris demanded. "So I'd go back into witness protection? Because that's not going to happen."

"You were just attacked by two Jackals!"

She glared at him. "What's to say you didn't lead them to me?"

He stepped back against the wall and gritted his teeth to keep from pointing out that wasn't possible. He'd spent his entire career infiltrating heinous organizations and he did it by remaining inconspicuous, not by getting himself followed by masked men. The only time he'd ever come close to blowing his cover was when he'd chased after the green-masked Jackal who'd been spying on her. And for all the criminal had known, Mack had just been a really concerned friend. He might not know Mack was a cop even now.

"If you knew Jackals were tracking me," she added, "why didn't you just arrest them?"

"Because, one, even if that was as easy as you just made it sound, I'm not the kind of cop who does the arrests," he said. "I'm the undercover kind who pretends to be a really, really bad guy in order to gather the evidence needed for other cops to sweep in and arrest the real bad guys. I pretend to be the kind of man you'd never want to meet." And that was a side of him he hoped she'd never see. "That means never blowing my cover. Second, I hadn't actually seen either of those Jackals this time around, until one of them was attacking and sedating me, and once that happened, keeping us both alive became the highest priority. And trust me, I'd have known if I was being followed. Finally, I've been suspended—"

Mack cut his eyes to the walls around him to keep from having to meet her gaze in the darkness. But it didn't prevent him from hearing Iris gasp as if someone had knocked the air from her lungs.

"The night we last saw each other," he said slowly, "there was a Jackal in a green, camo-colored mask hanging around outside your apartment. He was looking in your bedroom window, holding a tranquilizer gun. I was pretty sure he was going to abduct you." He huffed out a breath. "Also, I'm fairly certain it was the same one who attacked us back at the diner. I don't tend to forget anyone I've tangled with, even if they're masked. From hands to build to shoulders to voice, there are a lot of ways my brain tends to remember people like that beyond just their face. Anyway, I wasn't supposed to engage, not unless your life was in imminent danger. But instead I chased him down and got shot for my trouble. I'm under internal review as to what went wrong. I'm not allowed to do anything to impact the Oscar Underwood investigation. And I only retained my authorization to carry a gun due to the sheer number of criminals out there who want me dead."

He resisted the urge to point out she'd been running pretty close to the gray line of Canada's handgun laws when she'd pulled a weapon on him for startling her earlier, not that he suspected any right-thinking officer would prosecute her over it.

"So you weren't assigned to track me down?" she asked.

"No," he admitted. "In fact, coming to find you like this could further complicate my suspension. But I'm hoping if any of the higher-ups are unhappy with me for looking for you, the fact that I was actually able to find you and hopefully get you back into witness protection and in court for Oscar Underwood's trial will smooth that over."

"And if I don't go back into witness protection?" she asked.

Then I risked my badge for nothing but the knowledge you were okay. The words crossed his mind, but he stopped himself from speaking them. "At least we'll know that we're each safe and still alive, and maybe this time we can say goodbye properly."

Sudden light flooded the camper as if someone was shining a bright light in every window at once.

"Get out of the camper! Hands up!" The voice was male, loud and exuded the kind of malice Mack had heard too many times before. "Now! Or we're coming in!"

FOUR

Instinctively, Mack pressed himself back against the wall and glanced through the camper curtains. The light was no longer shining directly in the windows, and he could now see there were two men, both clad in bulky winter jackets and jeans. They looked exactly like the kind of guys he'd expect to see prowling around the perimeter of a rural complex in the middle of nowhere, except for the most certainly illegal high-powered rifles in their gloved hands.

The younger one was bald with several badly drawn facial tattoos and the overall impression of a man in his early twenties struggling in all the wrong ways to find his place in the world. The other was the scarred and scowling face of Eddie Paul, a volatile thug for hire who specialized in taking on head-of-security gigs for bigger criminals and had a string of violent assault charges to his name.

It had been years since Mack had exchanged blows with Eddie, in a very different place and when Mack had been under an extremely different guise. But

Mack had never been one to forget a face. Or a rap sheet.

As far as he knew, a memory for people was the one positive thing he'd inherited from his incredibly wealthy and strict father—a man who'd terrified Mack as a child, saddened him as an adult and had taught him at a young age that pretending to be someone he wasn't was sometimes the best means for survival. Mack's father was one of the country's most successful businessmen in part because of his uncanny ability to never forget the face, name or story of anyone he'd ever met. Mack's mother might be good at making friends, but his father, it was said, could walk into any major business, office building, golf course or country club and find someone there he'd met before.

Mack was the same. Only instead of receptionists and CEOs, he had an encyclopedic memory of criminals.

Lord, I could really use some wisdom right now. Because none of the ways I can think of to get out of here alive involve anything I want to do in front of Iris.

Iris glanced past him, brushing his shoulder as she peeked into the gap he'd made in the curtains.

"Wow, I'm sorry," she said, with way less fear than the situation deserved. "Looks like I found another really bad place to park. I'm just going to pop out and apologize to them and then we can hit the road."

His jaw dropped. Was she kidding him with this? Every hair at the back of his neck was warning him of danger, and here she was like a little mouse that had blithely wandered into the lion's den and figured she'd just say sorry and continue on her way. The crazy thing was that, knowing Iris, it would probably work, as long as the men didn't peek into the camper and find him there.

Mack took her hand in his and pulled her away from the window.

"That might actually work—for you," he whispered. "You've got this really sweet but no-nonsense way about you that makes people want to give you a break. No matter how criminal someone is, they're still human. But I've tangled with one of those two men before. His name is Eddie Paul, and he was betrayed once by one of my cover identities named Graves."

Graves was a particularly unpleasant person whom Mack had hated assuming and been very thankful to "kill off" a year ago.

"The only reason Eddie hasn't tried to kill Graves," he added, "is that he thinks I'm already dead."

The good news was that Eddie was savvy enough to prefer threats and very targeted attacks over murder. He was unlikely to kill Iris unless ordered to by whomever he was working for now. The bad news was that Eddie wasn't the kind to let her go without first searching her camper, and when he suddenly came face-to-face with Mack, it wasn't going to go well.

"I said, open up!" Now the shouting was accompanied by a loud rap on the camper door.

Iris darted forward, pulling out of his grasp and stepping toward the door. "One moment!" she shouted back. "Just give me a second!"

"What are you doing?" Mack whispered. He reached for her arm to pull her back and missed.

She stepped close to him and kept her voice low. "I'm stalling them."

She was what? His jaw dropped. He was the cop, she was the civilian and it was his job to get her out of there alive. "Don't," he said.

"Don't what?"

"Don't do anything," he whispered. Another burst of knocking erupted on the door outside. "You may have stumbled through any number of incredibly dangerous situations in your life and made it out alive. But right now, it's my job to keep you safe."

"Okay," she whispered. "I'm listening. What do you need to do that?"

A moment to think, information about what kind of operation he'd stumbled into and to somehow stop the erratic pounding in his heart that seemed to happen whenever Iris was near.

Iris's chin rose. Her face was pale, but defiance and strength filled her eyes. He couldn't imagine how hard she was working to hold her tongue and let him think. She was one of the most genuine, compassionate and well-meaning people he knew. She also always wanted to talk.

Silence had fallen outside the camper. Her stalling tactic seemed to have bought them a moment. But he needed far more than that. They were worse off than fish in a barrel.

"Well, what do you want to do?" she asked.

Scoop you up into my arms and run to safety. "I want to talk to my team," Mack said.

"Okay," she said. "Then how about I walk out there, apologize very profoundly and loudly and distract them for you while you talk to your team?"

"No. Because they might hurt you," he whispered as loudly as he dared.

"Not immediately," she said. "It's not like they want to kill me, they just want to scare us off. And if bad things start to go down, you can jump out and have my back. It's also possible they'll just yell at me and let me go."

He hated every single thing about that plan, including the fact it was exactly the kind of thing he'd have come up with if Iris had actually been a member of his team and his chest didn't ache at the thought of her being in danger.

The banging started up again, followed by the rattling of someone shaking the door.

"What's going to be worse for me?" she asked. "If I go out there and stall them while you make a plan? Or if they burst in here and shoot us both?"

He took a deep breath and prayed. He couldn't believe he was doing this.

"Go," he whispered. "Quickly, before I change my mind. Talk up a storm. Be loud and dramatic. Distract them as long as you can, and if they agree to let you drive off, all the better. But whatever you do, don't lie to them. I know you probably think people have been believing whatever cover story you've been giving them so far. But I'm guessing they just thought you're a really nice person in trouble and they wanted to help you. Trust me. You're a terrible liar."

Her eyes opened wide. In a life full of fake people and criminals, Iris was the most real person he'd ever met.

"If anything happens I'm coming out, guns blazing," he added. "If they so much as lay a hand on you or try to take you anywhere, I'm throwing the plan out the window and coming after you. You're not alone. You got that? Not even for a second. I've got your back."

"Enough stalling!" Eddie's fist banged the door. "I'm counting to ten and then I'm shooting the lock off the door! One. Two—"

"I'm coming!" Iris flung the door open and stepped out so quickly Mack barely had time to press back against the wall. The door clicked shut behind her. "Hello, hey, guys! Wow, I'm so sorry, I didn't mean to cause any trouble. I got all turned around looking for a place to stop. Are those guns real?"

Nice. He couldn't have thought of a stronger opening. She sounded confused, apologetic and eager to resolve this whole thing as quickly as possible.

He dropped to the floor, pulled out his phone, clipped an earpiece into his ear and activated the encrypted video messaging system that Seth had set up for them.

"Hey." Liam Bearsmith's deep voice filled his ear. Mack glanced down at the video on his phone. The relentless, broad-shouldered undercover detective was crammed at a small desk, just to the right of spiky-haired hacker Seth. "Did you find Iris?"

"Does she like your beard?" Seth asked.

"See, I'm driving across Canada…" Iris's voice filtered through the door "… I didn't really have a plan…"

Iris was still talking and not letting either of the gun-toting men get a word in edgewise.

Found her. Mack typed his response into the video's chat feature. What can you tell me about a place called Crow's Farm and why a criminal like Eddie Paul would be patrolling the perimeter?

Liam didn't even pause. "Crow's Farm is the code name of Alexis Corvus's new drug operation. That is if the chatter I've been chasing is to be believed, but my sources tend to be solid. It's off the grid. No one knows where it is or what exactly he's cooking. Just that he either paid or killed off everyone involved with taking down his last operation."

Whoa. Alexis Corvus was a medium-size shark in North America's drug operations. Mack had tangled with him a couple of times in the past as Graves. As far as Corvus was concerned, he'd successfully had Graves killed. Looked like Mack was about to disappoint.

"Who's in the camper?" Eddie barked at Iris.

Yeah, the stall tactics weren't going to last much longer. Time for a new plan and fast.

"Why?" Liam asked.

I think I'm accidentally there now, Mack typed.

Liam whistled under his breath.

Iris created this giant roadmap, Mack went on, of hundreds of purported safe places in the country that she heard homeless street youth talk about.

"And how many are criminal organizations?" Seth asked.

Mack didn't know. But he did know that a criminal like Eddie seeing the map could put Iris's life in even more peril.

"Locking onto your GPS coordinates," Seth said. "Locating you on satellite. Downloading everything."

"I asked you who's in the camper!" Eddie's voice rose outside.

"You know what?" Iris still sounded confused. "To be completely honest, I don't really know. You'd think I would. But he's given me two completely different stories so far. He collapsed in a parking lot, I felt bad just leaving him there and since then, pretty much all he's done is sleep."

Mack's eyes cut to the door. There was only one good way out of this. And it meant showing Iris a side of himself that he really didn't want her to see. Once he showed her, there'd be no going back.

But if her life was on the line...

Mack snapped a picture of the map, including the pictures from the homeless center surrounding it, sent it to Seth, then ran his sleeve across the laminated map, reducing her hard work to nothing but smears.

"Open the door!" Eddie barked.

"Wait!" Iris said. "You can't!"

"Get out of the way," he snapped. "Bud, if she moves shoot her."

"Pray for me, guys," Mack said. "I'm going in."

He grabbed the door handle. *Here goes nothing.*

He prayed, swallowed hard and felt his cover identity click into place.

"Hold your horses, dude!" he bellowed. "I'm coming."

Iris's frantic heart beat through her chest so hard it hurt to breathe. For an instant, she thought she'd seen something—like a mixture of amusement and pity—flicker in the face of the silent, bald, tattooed young man called Bud that made her think they might just let her go. But the ugly, scarred brute who was now practically shoving her out of his way was a whole other story.

Eddie yanked at the door. It didn't open. Mack must've locked it from the inside.

"Enough stalling." Eddie turned and aimed his weapon between Iris's eyes. "Everybody inside that camper better get out here now or I'm shooting your lady."

The door flung open with such force that it smashed back against the camper wall. A gasp fell from Iris's lips, barely more than a whimper, as she saw the hulking man who stood there, defiant and scowling. He filled the doorway of her little camper.

Mack?

"What's your problem?" growled the man who was Mack and yet nothing like Mack. "I told you I was coming. The lady told you I wasn't feeling a hundred percent. And yet you kept on banging."

"Graves…" Eddie uttered the name like it was something even worse than a swear word and his face went white. Iris couldn't tell if he was more angry or terrified to see Mack standing there.

A snarl curled Mack's lips. Dark circles under narrowed eyes crowded out the blue of his irises, his hair was disheveled, and the jagged edges left by the prosthetics glue were somehow even dirtier than before and looked like scars. He strode out of the camper and that's when she noticed… Thick black smudges ran down his right sleeve and over the fingers of his left hand.

The camper door swung shut, but not before she saw the black and blue smears that were all that remained of her map of safe places.

What had he done?

Mack cut his eyes to the guns Eddie and Bud were pointing at her head and groaned. "Are you kidding me with this?" he said. "She's not my lady. She'd just a nice person who went out of her way to help a guy in trouble."

How could Mack—or anyone, for that matter—just switch their demeanor and identity like that? Yes, earlier in the camper when they'd been arguing, it was like he'd suddenly straightened his back and draped the mantle of being a cop around his shoulders. But this new identity wasn't an addition. It was more like he had somehow squelched all his soft, compassionate parts, leaving nothing but this surly stranger behind.

For a long moment Eddie just stood there, gaping at him, like someone had put him on pause. Then he stepped back like he'd just been punched. He glanced at Bud and both of their guns swung around and pointed at Mack.

"You've got to be kidding me with this," Eddie said. "You're supposed to be dead."

Mack raised his hands half-heartedly and laughed. "If it helps any, I was legally dead for a couple minutes, but it didn't take."

It was funny how tone could change everything. When Mack had said almost the exact same words to her earlier, there'd been something almost endearing about them, like he'd was trying to make a joke to be reassuring. Now they were laced with a defiance that was anything but.

"And please tell Corvus I don't think much of his welcome."

"He's expecting you?" Eddie asked.

"No." Mack shrugged. "I just heard about your little drug operation a few minutes ago and decided to come for a visit."

Eddie's eyes narrowed. "I don't believe you."

"Because you're so well hidden no one can find you?" Mack crossed his arms. "I'm done talking until you take me to Corvus."

What did he mean, take him to Corvus? No, they were leaving. Now. And together.

"Thanks for the ride." Mack waved the back of his hand at her like she was nothing but a buzzing fly. "But I can take it from here. You can go."

The barrel of Eddie's gun swung toward her. "She's not going anywhere."

"Oh, really?" Mack stepped forward until his chest was bumping against the weapon in Eddie's hand. "'Cause you want to sour my meeting with Corvus right off the bat by making problems for me? Or are you going to skip the meeting so you can teach Bud here just how hard it is to make a woman's body, a big truck and a camper disappear so nobody's ever going to find it? Think!" His voice grew to a frustrated roar. "A person like her has dozens of people who'll plaster her face all over TV if she goes missing. You really think she's gonna drive two hours to town and convince a bunch of cops to come back here just because a couple of big scary men got into a yelling match about things she don't understand?"

He brushed past Eddie and Bud as if their weapons weren't pointed at him and walked over to her, placing himself between her and them. He looked down at her. Something soft she couldn't place pooled in the blue of his eyes. His hand landed on her shoulder and gently squeezed twice. Her chest tightened around her heart until she was unable to breathe. While Mack's words were directed to the criminals around them, his eyes were locked on hers and hers alone.

"Nah, see, this is just a really sweet girl," Mack said. "The kind every man hopes to meet but never really expects to find. She just made the mistake of trusting a man she doesn't know. She told me all about her life, her parents, her three older siblings and her nieces and nephews, and how she'd do anything to keep them safe."

She opened her mouth, but no words came out. His fingers brushed the side of her face until they rested under her chin. He tilted her face up until she was looking right into his eyes.

"Now, look," he said, "you're going to get into your truck, right now, and drive. You're not going to stop. You're not going to look back. You're not going to ever come back here. Got it? You're going to forget you ever met me. If I want to find you, I will."

She knew his words probably sounded like a threat to the criminals. Yet as she looked in his eyes, she heard something else. An apology? A final goodbye? But he didn't mean what he was saying, right? He wasn't really asking her to leave him there, with criminals who wanted to kill him, take off running and never see him again. There had to be another way. Still, she couldn't help but hear the undeniable ring of truth.

"I don't understand…" she whispered, so softly she could barely hear her own words.

"You don't need to understand, you just need to do what I say." Mack's voice rose. "Got it?"

She nodded as sudden tears filled her eyes. "Yeah. Yeah… I got it."

He was putting his life on the line to save hers, knowing it might mean they never saw each other again.

"Good." He stepped back. "Get out of here. Don't make me regret my decision." His hand slid to the small of her back, lingered there for a moment, and then he pushed her toward the truck so sharply her knees almost buckled. "Don't look back."

"Do you know what you're doing?" Eddie's voice came from somewhere behind her.

"Of course I do," Mack snapped. "I'm getting rid of a problem the smart way. There's a reason I got hired on the Quebec job, not you. I don't go around creating unnecessary messes."

She stumbled to the truck. Unshed tears clouded her vision. Her limbs trembled as she climbed into the driver's seat, her keys shaking so hard in her hands she could barely slide them into the ignition. The truck purred to life. The headlights cut a path in the darkness. She glanced in the side mirror. They were already leading Mack away.

She drove, pushing through the trees and pulling the camper behind her.

This couldn't be happening. Jumbled prayers poured through her heart, begging God to save Mack. He'd searched for her and found her. He'd been shot trying to save her life twice; first when he'd been undercover as a volunteer and just tonight with a tranquilizer dart back in an empty gas station parking lot. How could she just leave him, alone and helpless with criminals who wanted him dead, knowing she might never see him again?

Something buzzed in her jacket pocket and then an unfamiliar ringing filled the truck. She pulled over near the complex wall and searched for the source of the sound.

There was an unfamiliar, slim, silver phone in her right pocket. She yanked it out and answered the video call.

A thin man with messy hair appeared, sitting at a keyboard. A petite and smiling blonde woman flanked him on one side, and a large, stern-looking man sat on the other.

"Iris James?" The intimidating man spoke first. "I'm RCMP Detective Liam Bearsmith. This is Detective Jessica Eddington and computer expert Seth Miles. Welcome to the team."

FIVE

What team? Mack's team? When had Mack slipped a phone in her pocket? She cut the engine so there would be no interior or headlights to draw unwanted attention and let the falling snow beat unabated against the windshield.

"Well, you clearly know who I am," she said, feeling her chin rise. "I'm guessing you're that special detective team that's going around finding people who might not actually want to be found and trying to talk them into letting you protect them."

Seth snorted, and Jessica hid a smile behind her hand. Only Liam's mouth didn't twitch.

"Pretty much," Liam said. "Although we wouldn't put it quite like that."

"I like her description better," Seth interjected.

"So I guess that means you know I'm outside Crow's Farm," Iris went on, "a place run by some guy called Corvus with henchmen named Eddie Paul and Bud, who I'm pretty sure want to kill Mack. Well, they've got Mack and we need to rescue him."

None of them looked the slightest bit surprised by this.

"Got it," Liam said. "Right now, we need you to get out of there as quickly as you can and make it to a safe house. Seth is searching for the coordinates of one now and will get them to you in a moment. From there, we'll arrange for an officer to extract you and take you back into witness protection."

"No." She shook her head. "Didn't you hear me? Very bad people have Mack. I'm not just going to drive off and leave him to fend for himself." Even if that was exactly what he'd told her to do.

"I understand—" Liam began.

"Do you?" Iris demanded. "Because a member of your team has just walked inside a very scary-looking walled complex. And you're sitting there like that just happens every day."

Liam leaned back in his seat and crossed his arms. "I promise you that Mack means a lot to all of us, and we're every bit as worried about him as you are. But going into very scary-looking places at gunpoint with really bad people who want to kill him is kind of Mack's specialty," he said. "And right now, my first priority is making sure you live to testify against Oscar Underwood."

"How did he walk in there?" Jess asked.

"He was pretending to be an arrogant, snarly man—"

"Graves?" Jess interjected.

"Yeah." Iris nodded. Mack had told her she wouldn't like the kind of man he'd pretended to be. He wasn't wrong. "He told Eddie he wanted a meeting with Corvus."

Liam and Jess exchanged a look. It spoke volumes from a library she was locked out of. Seth was still typing, but it didn't matter what address he found. She wasn't about to run anywhere and leave Mack behind until she was convinced it was the right thing to do.

"Don't worry," Seth said. Something in his tone made her think he was trying to take his own advice. "Mack is really hard to kill. He'll be back, sooner or later. I'm sure of it."

Easy for him to say.

"Who exactly is Graves?" Iris asked.

"Max Graves is one of Mack Gray's cover identities," Liam answered. "Mack used him to infiltrate and take down several criminal enterprises over the years before we arranged to have him killed off."

Iris took a deep breath and asked the question she wasn't sure she wanted an answer to. "Is Graves a killer?"

"No." There was a weight to the single word Liam said. "Graves was a middleman and security expert who specialized in getting hard-to-obtain things, especially information. But the most important thing to know is that no matter what cover identity Mack took on, he was always still a good man at heart. He always held on to his faith in God, looked out for the underdog and did whatever it took to see justice done and protect those in need."

"And," Jess added, "for whatever it's worth, you should know he really cared about you."

Iris wasn't sure what to make of that. "Then how about we stop talking about my running away to a safe house, and you tell me how we're going to save his life."

Seth's computer pinged. "Got it!" he said. "I'm sending you the coordinates now."

Almost immediately a link to a map popped up on the phone screen. She swiped it away. "I'm telling you, I'm not just running away, bailing on Mack and leaving him here to die."

"Look." Something hardened in Liam's eyes. He leaned forward, his elbows resting on the table. "First off, we've been saving each other's lives from far more difficult and dangerous situations long before you even met Mack and we're not about to abandon him now. And second, this is who Mack is. This is what Mack does. He wears the identity of a criminal in order to infiltrate really bad places and get information to other cops who sweep in, take down the bad guys, get the limelight and the praise."

Iris suspected that description applied to Liam and the rest of them, too.

"Whatever he's doing inside Crow's Farm," Liam said, "he'll also believe God led him there and that he has a job to do. Good will come of this."

If he survived. "But this wasn't a planned operation," she said. "He pretended to be Graves and let himself be taken at gunpoint to meet with Corvus in order to protect me."

"I get that," Liam said, "and sometimes in this business, we wing it. In fact, we wing it a lot." He closed his eyes and she had the suspicion he was praying.

When he opened his eyes, he said, "Okay, here's how this is going to go down. We're going to send someone we trust to camp outside Crow's Farm, to be there to pick Mack up when he inevitably finds a way to escape on his own. While they're there, they'll also do a surveillance of the property—its security measures, entrances and exits, all that stuff—in case we need to arrange an extraction."

Iris closed her own eyes a moment and prayed. She didn't know what it was inside her that was so determined not to just run, save herself and leave Mack behind—especially after seeing the kind of man he pretended to be and discovering their past friendship had been nothing but a cover story. Maybe it was just the inbuilt thing inside her that made it impossible to turn away from anyone in trouble. But it felt like something else, something stronger, and whatever it was, she wasn't about to ignore it now.

"Then that's what I'll do," Iris said. "I'll stick around here a little while, just in case Mack manages to escape. While I'm at it, I'll send you some intel about the place to help you plan an extraction."

She didn't know exactly how long or short a time that was going to be, or what she was going to do if Mack didn't come out running. But she'd cross those bridges when she came to them.

"I can't authorize that," Liam said.

"I know," Iris said, "and I'm not asking you to. But it's my life and I'd rather take it into my own hands to help someone…" *who matters to me in a way I can't begin to explain* "…than just run away without at least trying to help him." She unbuckled her seat belt. "I can take pictures by clicking the picture icon on the bottom of my screen and the pictures will show up at your end, right?"

"Yup," Seth said.

"I'm going to climb a tree and take some pictures of the complex." Just sitting in the truck doing nothing was going to make her absolutely stir-crazy. Sitting still had never been one of her strong suits. She whispered another prayer, took a deep breath and opened the door.

"Stay in the vehicle, Miss James." Liam's tone was stern, but still there was something reassuring about his voice that she liked. In a different time and place, she'd have probably been happy to follow his direction and been glad to be on this team. "Please leave the area, head to the location you've been sent and we'll send an RCMP officer to rendezvous with you. Now, confirm you've heard me."

"Yup, I've heard you, but I'm not changing my mind." She leaped out of the truck and into the snow. "Worst-case scenario, if something goes incredibly wrong, how long will it take to scramble a team, or whatever it is you do, to extract me?"

"Don't answer that—" Liam started.

"Forty-eight minutes," Seth said, "and that's a long time to stay alive if they take you hostage."

"Good thing I'm not going to get captured then," she said. "I'm just going to stay outside the complex, take a few pictures of the place to help you get the intel you need to rescue Mack, and then I'm getting out of here." Hopefully with Mack. She slid the phone into her breast pocket. "Back in a second."

"I like her," Seth said, seemingly to no one in particular. "She's got spunk."

She reached into her pocket and muted the volume, leaving the video chat open. Then she started along the wall, looking for a solid tree to climb or a gap to look inside.

Yeah, she'd been accused of having "spunk" before, along with being labeled stubborn, difficult, strong willed and even a brat when she was younger. Her mother liked to joke that her first "word" had been "No-I-do-it-myself!" Iris preferred to think of it as determination, as well as an unrelenting inability to ever turn her back on an underdog.

Okay, sure, maybe hanging around in the woods outside the complex where Mack had been taken was a bad idea. But it's not like she had any really good options, was it? She didn't exactly trust the cops to protect her from Underwood's Jackals, Mack had erased her map of potential safe places and she couldn't contact anyone from her past or family for their safety.

Not to mention something in her heart wouldn't let her run without at least trying to help Mack.

A tree loomed ahead, thick, broad and growing close to the wall. Its branches were so heavy with snow they pressed down on the barbed wire on top of the wall, like a natural bridge. She pushed through the needles and sharp empty twigs that lay closest to the trunk and started climbing, staying close to the trunk as she grabbed branch after branch. Seemed some childhood skills never left a person.

It wasn't until she was in social work that she'd realized just how much she'd taken for granted. Not everyone got nothing but a stern talking to when they'd cut class to help out a friend in need, raided the food that was supposed to be for dinner to give to someone who was angry or scaled a farm fence to try to rescue a chained-up dog. As a teenager, her inability to let even the smallest injustice go by without confronting it had led to her getting fired from job after job, and one of her older brothers and his wife had taken her in to live on their farm over a summer and hired her to take care of their kids. She'd been surrounded by love, understanding, grace and forgiveness. As she'd told Mack when they'd compared childhood stories, there was more than one way to be rich.

If Mack hadn't warned his team that she wasn't the type to stay put and do what she was told when someone she cared about was in danger, then he didn't know who he was dealing with.

She reached the top of the wall. It was about ten feet tall, she guessed, but seemed shorter thanks to the several feet of soft snow that had fallen on both sides. She could probably leap down and land safely inside the complex, if she'd wanted to. Thick branches bent low over the top, flattening the thick barbed wire. But she wouldn't be much of a farm girl if she didn't know how to handle a barbed wire fence. She stepped forward, keeping one foot on the tree and placing the other one on the wall, knocking the snow off the branch as she went.

A smattering of buildings lay inside the complex. There was a large brick building that seemed to be part greenhouse to her right. Through the foggy glass she caught glimpses of red and pink. Then she saw him.

Mack was down on his knees. A thin, bearded elderly man, who she guessed was Corvus, stood in front of him. Eddie stood behind him, his gun aimed at the back of Mack's head.

Her mouth went dry. Her legs shook. There was no time for the RCMP to mount a rescue. Corvus's men were going to execute him. They were going to kill him, and there was nothing she could do to save him.

Holding tight to the tree with one hand, she wordlessly eased her phone out of her pocket and pointed it toward the scene, praying that somehow, Mack's team would see something that would help them save his life.

Lord, please, don't let Mack die like this.

She stepped forward, crouching low and letting go of the tree, as she braced herself against the wall. The branch snapped back, lifting off the wire now that it was no longer weighed down by either her foot or the snow.

Sudden sirens filled the air. Spotlights spun. Electricity shot through her feet, immobilizing them and filling her body with pain. Her knees buckled, and a scream tore from her lips as she pitched forward and fell into the complex.

Mack thought he'd heard a scream, a singular noise that somehow rose above the wailing of the sirens. But right now all that mattered was the gun to his head and the fact he suddenly had a very handy distraction.

He barely had time to drop before he heard the deafening blast of a gunshot split the air where his head had just been. He reared up and threw himself at Eddie, knocking him to the ground, and grabbed for the gun. He wrestled the weapon from the criminal's hands, then ducked the desperate sucker punch Eddie threw at his head. Mack rolled, kicking Eddie's feet out from under him before he even had the chance to stand. Mack had always been the stronger fighter. He'd had to be. It took a lot more skill and ability to avoid seriously hurting a person and yet still subdue them than it would take to actually do damage.

Sirens and lights were still blaring. As thankful as he was for the distraction, Mack prayed that it hadn't been Iris who'd tripped the security alarm or her that he'd heard scream.

He hadn't exactly had a plan for escaping when he'd decided the only way to save Iris's life had been to let Corvus capture him. He'd stashed his own gun in the camper, knowing that Eddie would search him and take it anyway. But he'd always been good at improvising. Not that he hadn't been hoping he'd be able to somehow talk his way out of the situation, instead of Corvus deciding a quick and simple execution was how he wanted to deal with Graves.

Now, Corvus had disappeared, having taken off running as soon as the alarm had sounded. And Eddie, now without his weapon, was stumbling to his feet in the snow, ready to take another try at bringing Mack down.

Mack took a step back and pointed Eddie's own weapon at him. "Don't be an idiot, man!" Mack shouted above the wailing sirens, in a tone that sounded like Graves and yet a sentiment he genuinely meant. "I don't want to hurt you, let alone kill you. I just want to get out of here! And you clearly got another situation you gotta go deal with."

Eddie snarled and charged.

Mack sighed and fired, clipping Eddie in the shin. The criminal bellowed in pain and dropped to the ground.

"Put some pressure on it!" Mack shouted and ran for the perimeter wall. "It's just a graze. The snow should help with the pain. You'll be fine."

Mack pelted through the snow toward the wall. Ironically the glaring spotlights would actually make him harder to see as long as he stayed in the shadows. He ran in a zigzag, staying low, keeping close to the edges of the maze of buildings and using the distraction of the security alarms and the lights to his advantage. Every investigative bone in his body wanted to search each and every corner of the complex to find out what kind of operation Corvus was running. But the part of him that wanted to live to fight another day was stronger.

Even stronger than that was the drive to see Iris again.

Her face filled his mind so suddenly he almost stumbled. The way she'd looked at him when he'd pretended to be Graves... He'd never wanted her to see that side of him. Graves was the personification of Mack's arrogance and anger. He was a reminder of who Mack would've become if he'd followed in his father's footsteps and not been found by God's love, forgiveness and grace. Would Iris ever look at him the same way now?

Just in front of the wall, a figure rose before him out of the snow. The indistinct form seemed squat and broad one moment and as tall and thin as a waif the next as the lights shifted over it. He raised Eddie's weapon, praying he wouldn't have to shoot. The figure's hands rose, empty and high.

"Mack! It's me!"

"Iris?"

He shifted his gun to the side and he reached for her, catching her around the waist with his empty arm and pulling her into his side. For a split second, Iris filled his senses and an odd warmth spread through his body. His heart beat faster and his lungs breathed deeper than they ever had before. Then he led her into the shadow of the nearest building and turned to face her.

"What are you doing here?" he asked. "How did you get in?"

"I fell off the wall! I think I set off the alarm by kicking off a branch that had disrupted the circuit."

"What were you doing on the wall?"

"Just standing on it."

"But why?"

"To see into the courtyard. So I could show your team what was going on."

He doubted his team would have asked a civilian to do that kind of surveillance and was incredibly certain they would have told her to head to a safe house. Mack himself had very directly told her to run and not look back. Instead she'd climbed the wall?

"What were you thinking?" he asked.

But she wasn't listening. She pulled away, dropped down onto her hands and knees and crawled back out into the snow.

"What are you doing?"

She didn't respond, and he wondered if she'd even heard him above the sirens.

He crouched down beside her in the snow. "Come on. We've got to go."

"I dropped your cell phone when I fell," she said. "I have to find it."

"It's okay." He reached for her hand but failed to catch it. "It's just a dummy device. It doesn't have any data on it."

"But your team called me on it," she said.

"Because I instructed them to!"

"I was shooting video for them," she told him, "so they could help you."

"Did they ask you to?" he asked.

She shook her head. He watched for a long moment as she searched the snow, listening to the sound of people shouting in the distance. The door of the closest building flew open with a bang. He flattened his body in the snow and prayed, pushing her down beside him and sheltering her with his arm as people ran past.

"I've got it," she said in his ear.

Thank You, God! "Where's the truck?" he asked.

"On the other side of the wall," she said. She slid the

phone into her pocket. "But the metal wiring on top of the wall is electrified."

Okay, so they had to find a way over the wall. He checked Eddie's gun and found it was out of bullets. He frowned, tossed it in the snow and glanced up at the building. The door was ajar and the building was only a few feet from the perimeter. There appeared to be skylights at the top to let in natural light. If they found a way to the roof, they could take a running leap and clear the wall, with several feet of snow to cushion their landing.

He scanned the courtyard. The coast seemed clear.

"Come on," he said. "This way."

He reached for her hand, she let him take it and he pulled her to her feet. They ran inside the building. He pushed the door closed behind them and the noise outside faded. Hot and muggy air surrounded them, so thick that for a moment he could barely breathe. A lush garden of huge deep red and fuchsia flowers lay ahead of them. Mack held a finger to his lips, she nodded and he led her to a narrow alcove behind what looked like the pipes of an irrigation system.

"Where is everyone?" Iris asked.

"A place like this won't have that many people," Mack said. "A couple dozen, if that. Maybe even less. Skeletal crews are easier to manage, especially when you don't want information leaking out. They have a lot of ground to cover looking for me."

Considering they were looking for Graves the criminal, and not Mack the detective, they'd be checking places filled with high-tech electronics and weapons before they searched the flowers.

Iris squeezed his hand, only lightly, but somehow the simple gesture sent shivers spreading through his core. It was only then he realized that they were still holding hands and that he wasn't in a hurry to let go.

"And we're back." Seth's sudden voice was faint but unmistakable.

Iris pulled her hand away from Mack's and fished the cell phone back out of her pocket.

"You still on the call with the team?" Mack asked.

"Apparently," she said. "But the screen was dead when I pulled it out of the snow. Guessing it came back to life."

He stepped toward her and glanced at the screen. Seth, Liam and Jess were still crowded around Seth's desk back at their safe house headquarters. The red icon in the corner of the screen indicated that battery was down to 20 percent.

"Probably a reaction to the extreme temperature," Seth said. "Gotta look into that later." He raised a hand in greeting. "Hey, Mack! Good to see you alive. See, Iris, told you he'd be back."

Iris smiled.

"Where are you?" Liam asked.

"Inside one of Crow's Farm's greenhouses looking at some very suspicious flowers," Mack said. "My top goal is getting Iris out alive. But we'll record everything we can as we go. Heads up though, the battery is pretty low, so it might cut out."

"Got it." Liam nodded.

"Just point the camera at stuff," Seth said. "I'll do the rest."

Mack held out his hand for the phone, Iris handed it to him and he slid it in his jacket's breast pocket, with the camera turned out toward the room. Then he started moving along the wall, gesturing at Iris to follow.

A field of flowers spread before them, wild and lush, in various shades of red, pink, lavender and mauve. He watched as her fingers darted out, stopping just inches away from touching the huge, serrated petals.

"They're gorgeous," she said, and he could almost hear her breath catch in her throat. "Do you have any idea what they are?"

"Opium poppies," he said. "Seth will be able to confirm it. Very illegal and used for making heroin."

"They're making homegrown heroin here?" she asked.

"Looks like it," he said. Would definitely explain the size of the operation and the level of security. "It's not an easy thing to make. Most street drugs are smuggled in. But our Vice squad's pretty good at catching that stuff at the border, so guess Corvus decided to innovate. Liam's probably tipping off the closest RCMP division as we speak. They'll get a warrant and raid the place. In forty-eight hours, all this will be gone and anyone still here when police arrive will be behind bars."

Some rural RCMP cops were going to get a career-changing bust on their record. He wished them well and prayed it all went down smoothly.

"No one will ever know you were behind it, right?" Iris asked. "You won't get any of the credit?"

He shrugged. "I mean, there's always a few people who know but undercover detective work isn't the kind of job you go into to get famous."

If he'd wanted his face and name splashed all over the media, he'd have kept his birth name of Mackenzie Gravenhurst, instead of changing it when he'd entered the police force. He'd have gone through life as the only child of wealthy couple Patrick and Annie Gravenhurst, who networked with important people and whose large donations got the family name stuck on things like parks, hospital wards and museum wings. But then Mack wouldn't be himself anymore. After helping take down dozens of organizations and hundreds of criminals, this would be just yet another arrest he'd know he had a small hand in.

But as he glanced at Iris's face, he saw something flicker in the depths of her hazel eyes he'd never expected to see—awe. Suddenly it hit him that this beautiful and tenacious woman standing here with him in a hothouse filled with illegal flowers had now seen several more sides of him than he'd ever let anyone see before. And even after all that, she'd scaled a wall to help him instead of turning her back.

He looked away quickly. Was it his imagination or was the air in there getting warmer?

Then he spotted a thin, narrow wooden trellis leaning up against the wall at the far end of the room. It wasn't a ladder, but it would do. He signaled for her to follow him and then, crouching low, he led her through the flowers until he reached the end of the row.

"We climb up there," he said, pointing. "Then we

open a skylight, run across the roof and jump over the wall. Got it?"

She nodded. "Absolutely."

He scanned her face. There wasn't even a flicker of doubt in her eyes. "You sure?"

"Yup," she said. "Sounds a lot easier than how I got in here. Who goes first?"

He frowned. He hadn't thought of that and didn't much like either option.

"I'll go," he said, making a snap decision. "Whoever's on that trellis is out in the open if someone comes in. I'll make sure it'll support our weight, that the window will open and the coast is clear. Then you'll climb up and join me on the roof." It was the best out of two terrible options, and it was amazing how much he hated the idea of leaving her side even for a moment. "Stay hidden and wait until I signal you, okay?"

"Will do."

His arms reached out to try to hug her before he even realized what he was doing. He pulled back at the last second and found himself awkwardly squeezing her shoulder instead. Then he darted out of the row of flowers, grabbed the trellis and started climbing. The structure shook under his weight, and he was thankful they hadn't tried to climb it together. As his eyes rose to the snow-covered glass above, he found himself struggling to keep from glancing back at the woman hiding in the flowers. He didn't know what this thing, this feeling inside him was. All he knew was that it was always there, distracting him, pulling him toward her, and he didn't know how to shake it.

He reached the skylight, forced the latch back and swung it open. Cold air and snow rushed in, as did the sound of sirens that still blared. He glanced down at Iris, and she flashed him a quick thumbs-up. Then he slid his body through the skylight and out. The wall was less than four feet from the edge of the roof.

He steeled his breath. He still had no idea why this detour had landed in their path or how he felt about Iris seeing this side of him, but he had to have faith that God would make something good come of it. Starting with the major drug bust some very fortunate RCMP officers were about to make.

But beyond that, his plans still hadn't changed. They'd escape, get somewhere safe, he'd somehow convince Iris to go back into witness protection and then they'd say goodbye and leave each other's lives forever. A man who did the kind of work he did didn't deserve a woman like Iris. She was worth far more than a life married to an undercover detective who disappeared for months at a time into criminal organizations. He had no idea how she'd react to knowing his parents were wealthy, but he knew just how much his father would turn his nose up at her. Mack wanted to spare her that, too.

Besides, was he even capable of living a life with his heart feeling this wide open and vulnerable all the time?

He glanced back down through the skylight and gestured at her to climb up and join him. She waved back, and a determined smile crossed her lips. And despite the way he knew it had to be, he still found himself wondering what it would've been like to spend the rest of his life with a woman who smiled like that in the face of adversity.

Iris darted from the flowers and ran for the trellis. Her hands grabbed the wood, and she started climbing. He heard a voice shouting below him. Then, as he watched, she froze and terror washed across her face.

Iris! Come on, keep climbing!

But she jumped down, her hands raised, and his heart stopped in his chest as he saw a second figure step into view.

It was Bud, the bald and tattooed young man who'd been outside with Eddie. He pointed a gun at Iris.

SIX

Fear filled Iris's veins as she stared into the pale eyes of the tattooed young man. She prayed he hadn't seen her looking up at Mack and that she hadn't blown Mack's cover.

"Please, don't shoot," she said, holding her empty palms up where he could see them. "I know I'm trespassing and I'm really sorry. But I honestly just want to leave. Like a lot. I climbed the wall to see if I could look in and see my friend. But then I accidentally triggered the alarm, the electric fencing at the top of the wall zapped me, and I fell in."

"You don't recognize me, do you?" he asked.

She blinked. Her eyes searched his face. "No, I really don't," she said. "Eddie called you Bud when you were both holding me at gunpoint outside the camper. But I don't know if that's your name."

"It'll do." Bud shrugged and the strap of his semi-automatic moved up and down on his shoulder. "I know you. You're that chick who runs the homeless center place in Toronto, right? They call you Missy?"

"Yeah…" Her heart switched from fear to regret in a beat. How would he know that? "I'm really sorry. I don't recognize you."

"Don't be sorry," Bud said. It was almost an order, like the fact she was now apologizing to him somehow bothered him. "I had a lot of long hair back then that covered my face and I didn't have these tattoos. Plus, I was wearing a hoodie. I remember that because there were signs telling me to take the hood off when I came into your place and I didn't. I came in for the community meal about six months ago. I was grabbing some food when some snitch told you I had a gun tucked under my shirt. You came over and told me I had to get rid of it. I told you the gun was a fake and that it couldn't even fire, but you said you didn't care. I could go put it in a locker at the front door or I could get out. Those were my options."

Yeah, she vaguely remembered that. It had been about two months before she'd met Mack.

"I'm sorry," she said. "Even if it wasn't a real gun, the rules are the rules."

"Stop saying that," Bud snapped. "You say sorry too much, you know that? And it wasn't a fake. It was real, and I was there because I had business with someone. But you didn't call the police on me and you let me take some food. You actually packed a bag of food for me yourself—like, a lot of food—and handed it to me all while making me leave. Plus you told me I could take some clothes from a bin on my way out. They were new. Never got new clothes from someone before." His shoulders rose and fell again. "You did me a solid that you didn't have to do. It reminded me of my mom. She was too nice and said sorry too much, too."

"Thank you," Iris said, not knowing what else to say. This wasn't the first troubled youth she'd met who'd blurted out some of his damage to her. Sometimes people who were hurt hid all the basic stuff— like name and age—but couldn't help but tell her the deeper stuff, like their parents' addictions or the fact someone they loved was in prison. He also wasn't the first who'd said she'd reminded them of a parental or authority figure, for good or for bad. Not even the first who'd been holding a weapon. And no matter what happened next, she still thanked God that she'd fed and helped him.

"Well, she's dead now," Bud said and as she watched, something went cold in his gaze. His chin rose. "She trusted the wrong people. But I got honor, even if some people don't. So I'm gonna return the favor and let you run, okay? Because Corvus will want you dead, and I don't kill people who don't deserve killing. Because I'm not that kind of person."

Like the person who'd killed his mother? Like someone else who'd once hurt him?

"Come with me," she said, "and I'll get you help. I'll help you get a good job, where you're not working for criminals. You can go to school. You can have a whole different and better life."

His eyes narrowed. "There's something really wrong with you, lady," he said. "You know that? You've got no sense of self-preservation. You can't just go around trying to help everyone else. Because one day you're going to try to help the wrong person and that'll be it for you."

"Maybe," she said, feeling something strong and fierce move through her heart. "But I can think of worse ways to go. I think I'm the way God made me to be, and I'm not going to stop being me just because someone's waving a gun at me."

Bud just shook his head. "Get out of here. Now. Before I get caught talking to you and we both get killed."

Fair enough. She walked backward to the trellis and felt the wood beneath her back.

"I heard about this place from some kids at the homeless center who were trying to escape Oscar Underwood and his Jackals," she said. "They said your boss wanted nothing to do with that whole kidnapping situation and only had people working for him who wanted to be. Not everyone who I think the Jackals nabbed were found. I feel like there was something else going on there and if I can find out where the others went, I can tip the police off so they can be rescued."

Bud's eyes narrowed. "Trust me, if the Jackals got them and they weren't working at one of Underwood's farms, they don't want to be found." He leveled the weapon at her. "Now go."

There was a shout from the other end of the building. "Hey, Bud!"

He turned. "Yeah?"

She started climbing the trellis, forcing her hands and feet faster and expecting any moment to hear a gunshot fire and feel a bullet pierce her skin. Then she felt a strong, warm, solid hand reaching for her. She grabbed hold of it and looked up into Mack's eyes as he pulled her through the skylight. She tumbled out onto the roof beside him, feeling the cold and wind lash her skin.

"I heard that." Mack's deep voice rumbled beside her. "You tried to talk a guy pointing a gun at you into escaping with us."

She nodded. Hot tears froze in the corners of her eyes. "I tried but I failed."

"You have no idea how absolutely incredible you are, do you?" He stood from his crouch, ready to sprint. "You ready to get out of here?"

"Yeah."

His fingers linked through hers. The warmth of his touch seemed to fill her body. She set her sights on the wall. They ran, hand in hand, until they reached the end of the roof. Then they leaped.

Mack's hands tightened on the steering wheel of Iris's truck as they drove through the night. Inky blackness filled the air outside, and the dashboard clock told him it was almost eleven. It hadn't even been five hours since he'd found her in the diner, and already they'd been through more in one evening than he had in any relationship he'd ever had with a woman.

She hadn't exactly liked the fact he'd insisted on driving. But considering how sore his body was from their jump over the wall, despite landing on a soft snowy cushion, he couldn't imagine how she felt having gone over the wall in both directions. That plus the argument about needing to evade any of Corvus's crew who might pursue them had seemed to finally win her over.

Thankfully they hadn't been chased. Probably because Corvus hadn't realized Mack had escaped the facility and still had his crew searching the grounds for a man who'd never really existed to begin with.

"You told Bud that some of the other street youth had told you about this place," he said, "and you asked if he knew where they were."

"Not everyone was found." Her slender shoulders rose and fell. "That means either they all escaped the Jackals and disappeared, or there are more kids out there waiting to be rescued."

"Is that what you've been doing while you've been on the run?" Mack asked. "Have you been looking for people?"

"No, not specifically," Iris said. "I'm not a cop, and I also still take seriously the fact I'm not supposed to be contacting people from my past. But I'm still keeping my eyes and ears open, just in case."

Yeah, he could respect that. Especially considering he'd come looking for her.

"I can't believe you destroyed my map," she said. "I'm sure you were just trying to keep Eddie from seeing it, but I don't know how I'm going to keep running without it."

Guilt stabbed his heart. Even now, Seth was pouring over it and would soon have an idea of which places were actually safe and which ones were criminal. Then Mack would have to figure out what to do with that information. He couldn't just let Iris keep running. It was too dangerous and there was just too high a risk of her being hurt.

But he couldn't just not tell her that he had a copy of her map. The only thing he could do was stall her just a little while longer while they regrouped with his team and he tried to make his case. If by sunrise he and his team hadn't managed to convince her, he'd give her Seth's annotated version of the map, free of possible criminal enterprises and traps, and let her go.

"I noticed you have pictures from the homeless center taped up in your camper," he said, extending the words like an olive branch. "You circled the faces of street youth we think the Jackals took but weren't found in the raids. If you'd like, I can ask Seth to run facial recognition software on your pictures of them. He might be able to tell you where they are now and even give you some peace of mind that they're safe."

"Thank you," she said. "That means a lot. I honestly don't know what to think of the fact that we stumbled upon a major crime operation and you just happened to know someone there."

He ran one hand over his head. "It would be stranger if I hadn't. It's like this. If I'd been a pro athlete for over a decade, I could probably walk into any major stadium in the country and run into someone that either myself, or someone I know, has played with or against. In every line of work, if you stay in it long enough and go deep enough, you keep running into the same people, or people you've at least heard of. I expect if I ever saw the green-masked Jackal without his mask on, I'd recognize him from some other past undercover case. Like my dad says, everything in life depends on networks."

"Your dad who was so poor that he emptied your bank account and stole your car and sold it?"

She shot the question at him so quickly he didn't have time to think up a deflection.

When he'd first been researching Iris, everything about her had made him think that the only child of a multimillionaire wasn't exactly the kind of person she'd naturally make friends with. Not that he'd ever asked his father for a single cent. She always said there was more than one way to be rich. Well, if growing up with his father had taught him anything, it was that there was more than one way to be poor.

A long pause spread thorough the truck. The windshield wipers beat against the snow. He braced himself for more questions about his father while he tried to figure out how best to tell her the truth about the huge house he'd been raised in that had never quite felt like a home.

Instead she asked, "Is Mack Gray even your real name?"

He blinked. "That's the name all my friends and fellow cops call me."

"I don't know why I didn't think to ask before," she said. "But until I saw 'Max Graves,' I didn't even think about the fact Mack might not be your real name."

Well, it wasn't the name he'd been born with. But Mackenzie Gravenhurst had been Mack to his friends ever since he was a teenager.

"Well, it is—"

"Why did you tell me your real name if we met while you were undercover?"

The force of her question struck him in the solar plexus and made him pause a moment.

"Mack Gray is a pretty generic name," he said. "There are dozens of Mack Grays in Canada and I'm not even the only one working for the RCMP. It was supposed to be a very low-profile assignment, and I didn't think there was much risk of you doing any kind of in-depth research into me and discovering I was a cop."

That was the answer he'd always given and the one that sprang immediately to his tongue. But was it the whole truth? Or had there been something else there, something about her, that had made him want to let her get to know the real him as much as he possibly could?

"Was everything about our friendship a fake from the very beginning?" she asked.

"What do you mean?" he asked.

"Like, we met at City Hall," she said. "I was camped outside Mayor Lisa Kats's office trying to get her to take action against Underwood. Her chief of security was practically trying to shove me out of the building and you stepped in. Was that staged?"

"His name was Travis Otis," Mack said, "and no, it was not staged. I looked in to him afterward and found out he'd violated parole conditions for a past aggravated assault and also had restraining order violations, as well. I tipped off a buddy about him, which got him arrested, which of course got him fired. But I'd been watching you for days, trying to find the right time to approach you. Travis was a brute and completely out of line, which gave me an opportunity to step in and help you."

And fake an accidental meeting.

The phone mounted on his dashboard started to ring. He'd logged off with his team after a quick check-in to let them know they'd made it safely to the truck. There were things his team had to do like search for data, and certain conversations they'd want to have without Iris listening in.

He answered the call. "Hello?"

"Hey." Seth sat alone at the desk now. There was a slight tightness to his smile. "So, I've found a new location to send you guys to. It's not a safe house, it's a camping site. It's called Stannum Campgrounds and I think you'll both be good with it."

"Really?" Iris asked. She glanced to Mack. "I think that placed was on my map."

"Mm hm." Seth nodded noncommittally, neither confirming or denying he'd ever heard anything about her having a map. "Yeah. It's got hills and a lake. It's remote, but good lines of sight. You guys can set up camp there and regroup."

It was a setup. Mack didn't have a moment's doubt about that. It was his team's way of giving him an opportunity to talk to Iris in private and figure out what to do from there. Most important, it would also at some point hopefully let Mack talk to them without Iris or anyone else listening in. As long as they were stuck together in the truck, she'd hear anything he said. And this way he could hopefully talk some sense into her before the next team call.

"I'm sending you the coordinates now," Seth added. "The campsite's very easy to get out of in an emergency and this way you can take turns getting some sleep while one of you keeps guard."

"Thanks," Mack said. "I really appreciate it. Just send me the coordinates, and I'll take it from there."

Seth had been a vigilante hacker, lurking behind a screen and taking down bad guys for years before he'd crossed the wrong criminal, ended up in witness protection and finally joined Mack's team. But he wasn't all that good at bluffing.

"Cool, will do," Seth said.

His finger reached to disconnect the call.

"Wait!" Iris said. "Seth! Can you do something for me?"

Seth paused and his eyebrow rose.

"I wasn't allowed to contact anyone from my life while I was in witness protection," she said. She glanced quickly to Mack and then back to the screen. "And I'm still completely respecting that. My family, friends and people who are running the homeless center agreed to respect that and not try to contact me, unless there was a really major emergency. Like a death or an illness. Would you be able to check my email inbox and let me know if there's anything important I need to know?"

Seth looked at Mack, who nodded. If Iris had stayed within witness protection—and hopefully when she went back into it—the officer assigned to her case would have helped create a safe conduit for her to find out significant information like that. Iris rattled off her email address and password.

"I'll give you a shout in a bit," Seth said. He disconnected.

"I don't mind if he reads my emails," Iris said, glancing at Mack. "I don't have any secrets and as for my personal life, I haven't been on so much as a coffee date since…"

She caught her words before she spoke them. But still he felt the end of the sentence floating in the air.

Since him and all the countless coffees, lunches and dinners they'd spent together. He'd come over to her apartment one afternoon and cooked her chimichangas, and they got brunch together so often their regular waitress had assumed they were married.

"How do you feel about the campsite idea?" Mack asked.

"There are a whole bunch of factors that come into play when I'm assessing the security of a place," Iris said. "I haven't just been running around willy-nilly into hotbeds of crime—"

"I never implied you had—"

"Like, was the location public enough that a Jackal wouldn't try to make an attempt on my life?" she went on, like he hadn't spoken. He still wasn't quite sure what to make of the edge to her voice, but it was growing stronger with every word. "And how easy would it be to escape? Stuff like that. And I figure as long as we don't allow us both to get trapped in the camper again, we should be okay. And I have no choice but to trust you until I sit down with my map and see how many places I can remember."

He turned toward her, but her eyes were fixed on the darkness outside.

"Look, I'm really sorry I wiped it like that," he said. "But like you guessed, I knew that if Eddie saw it, there was no way he'd believe you were just some random woman I ran across and let you go alive. Even at a glance, I could tell there were at least half a dozen criminal hot spots on it—"

"Out of hundreds of places—"

"One of which was an opium farm!"

"But they weren't all criminal organizations!" She turned back toward him, and something like defiance flashed in her eyes and spread through her voice. "Some were homeless shelters. Some were churches. Yes, I'm sure a few were guilty of paying people cash under the table. But it's just a coincidence that you were with me when I stumbled upon one that was an actual criminal enterprise."

He wasn't sure it was a coincidence though. He didn't believe in coincidences and something tingling at the back of his neck told him there was something else going on he couldn't see. Had it been God who'd led them there or something else entirely?

"I know you've spent your entire career dealing with criminals," she added. "But there are a lot of kind and decent people out there. People who gave me good honest work and others who let me camp on their property or gave me directions. Sure, some turned me away. But in my experience most people are good at their core and even those who are broken still have goodness in them."

He felt his hands want to rise defensively off the steering wheel. "I promise I'm really not attacking you."

"You heard what Bud said to me," Iris said. "He accused me of being naive and foolish and said that people like me got ourselves killed."

"Yeah," Mack said, "He said something like that. But he's clearly chosen a really bad path. So why care what he thinks? I don't believe any of that of you."

"How can you say that?" Iris asked incredulously. "You and I only know each other because you were undercover and I was your mark! You spent four months fooling me into thinking you were my friend, that you liked my company and wanted to be in my life."

Her words stung deeper than any bullet wound ever could.

"Is that what you honestly think?" he asked. "Seriously? I told you, over and over again, that I had a really hard time opening up to people and that I really liked spending time with you. Do you think those were all lies? Do you think I get super close to all my targets? Do you think I cook them dinner, stay late doing dishes with them, take them out for countless coffees and then chase them down across the country for weeks if they slip from witness protection? Because you're not the first pretty or interesting woman I've ever met while undercover. And you're not the first person to slip from witness protection under my watch. But you're the only one I put my life on the line to find."

Her mouth opened, and he could tell she was probably gearing up to say something. But this time, he didn't let her. He had something to get off his chest, even if he didn't quite understand why.

"I spent all that time with you and told you all those stories about my childhood because I liked you." His voice seemed to fill the truck despite his best efforts. "I liked spending time with you. I liked talking to you. You're interesting and funny and kind and sweet, and I couldn't get enough of your company. When you disappeared, I couldn't sleep without knowing you were okay. So yeah, I was undercover when we met. And yeah, when I told you stories about my life, I changed around a few names and places and disguised the specifics. But I opened up to you more than I've ever opened up to anyone, and I got closer to you than I've ever gotten to anyone, because I liked you and I liked spending time with you."

He stopped. He wasn't sure where all that had come from. Or what it was about what Iris had just said that had driven him so crazy. But the idea that she didn't get just how much she meant to him hurt, even if he didn't understand it himself.

He braced himself for her response, but for a long moment she didn't say anything. She just sat there in the truck, her eyes searching his face, and he had the unsettling feeling that somewhere in that whole avalanche of words he might've said something out of turn that he should be apologizing for.

The phone began to ring and he reached for it, thankful for the distraction. Seth's face appeared on the screen and somehow his smile was even tighter than it had been before.

"Hey, Iris," Seth said. "I checked your emails. Mostly coupons. Good news is your sister Alice is having a new baby in eight months, and your dad had a minor health scare but he's doing great now. Also, Mayor Lisa Kats of Toronto has been apparently trying to reach you to see if you wanted to hold a fund-raiser for your homeless center on her yacht."

Mack frowned. Mayor Kats was known for her lavish generosity to her own causes and also holding fund-raisers for others' charities on her expansive yacht. She had given dozens of young people full university scholarships and jobs training as part of her own program. It was one of the main selling points that had gotten her elected mayor and catapulted her to being seen as such a voice for helping the less fortunate.

"She's due to receive the Order of Canada from the prime minister next week," Mack told Iris. "Mostly for her personal charity work and scholarships, but also for what she's done for the city. Considering how many times you tried to meet with her about Underwood and the Jackals and she blew you off, I'm guessing she feels really foolish and wants to make it up to you."

"Or she feels guilty," Seth said. "The bad news is that three Jackals vandalized your homeless center last night."

She gasped. Mack felt his hand reach across the center of the cab and grab hers.

"No one was hurt," Seth said quickly. "They came in when it was empty. I only know they were Jackals because I saw the security footage."

"What did they destroy?" Iris asked.

"Everything." Seth swallowed. "It's all gone. They vandalized the entire place and then set the building on fire."

SEVEN

Mack watched as conflicting emotions flooded Iris's face. For a long moment she just sat there, with her hand in his and her lips slightly parted, until Seth awkwardly ended the call and said he'd talk to them later. Then she rolled down the window, stuck her head out into the cold, wintery night and screamed a long, loud warrior's yell, equal parts angry and defiant. When she stopped, she rolled the window back up, pulled her hand away from his and ran her fingers over her eyes.

He watched as prayers crossed her lips, asking God for wisdom and help. Finally she dropped her hands and turned to him.

"I'm sorry," she said. "But it was either that or burst into tears. And I was afraid that if I started crying I might never stop."

"Oh, Iris," Mack said. "I'm so sorry. I wish there was something I could do."

"Yeah," she said. "Me, too. I worked so hard to build that place up as a safe space and now it's gone. I tried everything I could to get people to believe Oscar Underwood's Jackals were real and kidnapping people, and now they've destroyed the homeless center. Not to mention how hard I fought to get the mayor to hear what I was saying about Underwood and the Jackals. And now that she finally wants to help, I'm not even allowed to contact her."

"Well, there's still hope, right?" Mack said. "After Underwood goes to trial and you testify, you might be able to go back to your normal life and rebuild the center the way you've always wanted."

"Can I?" Iris asked. "We assume that when Underwood goes to prison, his Jackals will stop working for him and stop trying to destroy my life. But what if they don't?"

"I don't know," he admitted.

The sign for the Stannum Campground loomed ahead in the headlight beams. The buildings at the front were closed for the off-season, and the entrance barrier was locked up in the open position.

Mack drove through, weaving his way through the campsites until he came to the one Seth had indicated. It was a wide, flat space, big enough for half a dozen tents or campers, with thick trees hemming it in on two sides. A steep hill flanked the other side, and faced a wide expanse of frozen lake. Perfect for a stealth aerial rescue if that's what he and the team decided on.

Mack parked the camper in the center. He busied himself building a fire in the firepit while Iris went inside the camper. He debated telling her that she should probably try to lie down and have a nap if she could, considering how late it was and that she must be exhausted. But knowing her she'd just insist she was fine.

He waited until the battery-powered lamp switched on inside before sending a quick message to his team, letting them know they were in position. He promised to call as soon as he knew that Iris had settled in for a while and he had time to talk uninterrupted.

Building campfires was something he'd always enjoyed—gathering materials, balancing the kindling just so, moving step by step, until he finally got to watch the fire burn.

But he hadn't gotten the opportunity to do it as much as he liked. His family had never gone camping as a kid. Instead, family holidays mostly involved going to very fancy places, where everything was uncomfortable and he wasn't allowed to touch anything, let alone get his hands dirty. His mother had tried her best to make it fun for the three of them. But even something as simple as swimming in the pool was under constant scrutiny by his father for "splashing too much," "just standing there wiggling his hands" or "not looking like he was having fun."

But hadn't that been his whole life? Being extra careful to keep up appearances and pretending very hard to be someone he wasn't just to get by?

Iris still hadn't emerged by the time the fire was ready to light, and he found himself lingering a long moment, watching as her shape passed back and forth past the windows. He even went as far as pressing his palms to his knees and standing up to go knock on the camper door before coming to his senses and sitting back down.

If he missed her so much when she was a few feet away, how was he going to manage when the team figured out their extraction plan and she left his life for good?

His phone told him it was nearing midnight. He frowned. It also showed that the phone hadn't actually been charging while they'd been driving, and the battery was now lower than ever. He fished a gas station receipt and lighter from his jacket pocket, set the paper alight and then nestled it inside the campfire. He blew on it gently and watched as the blue and orange flames spread to the twigs and brush around it. Then he sat back and let the snow fall on his face and the smell of smoke and pine fill his lungs.

His phone pinged with a message. It was Liam, telling him to get somewhere alone and then call him ASAP.

The sound of the door opening turned his attention back to the camper. Iris stepped out, holding the battery-operated lamp, and now he could see just how battered, scraped and damaged the walls of the camper had gotten since he'd found her less than six hours ago.

Iris stood there for a moment, bathed in the light of the lamp in her hand. In the other, she held a bottle of water. She'd changed her clothes and was now dressed in a clean pair of jeans and a soft blue turtleneck sweater under a puffy winter coat. And he knew without a shadow of a doubt that she was the most beautiful and fascinating person he'd ever seen in his life, even if he'd never be able to tell her that.

She walked toward him and it was like the heat of the fire grew with every step she took. His legs ached to stand, and his arms ached to open and pull her into his chest.

His phone pinged again, with a message from Liam that was just one word long: Important.

He typed, One second, and slid the phone back into his pocket.

She handed him the water, waited until he'd taken a long swig and then pulled a granola bar from her jacket pocket and handed it to him, too. Grateful, he unwrapped it and took a bite.

"Tell me you've eaten and drunk something, too," he said.

"I have," she said. "I've been trying to recreate the map from memory. But it's no use. For weeks, I've had options and been able to make a plan. Now the best I can do is shoot off into the dark and hope I land somewhere safe."

Or she could give up running altogether, let him bring her in and then let Jess help her build a new life. He finished the granola bar in two bites, stuffed the empty wrapper in his pocket and took another swig of water. He debated telling her that Seth had a copy of the map right away, but instead decided it made more sense to wait until after he'd talked to his team. He'd tell her very soon, just not right now.

She frowned, and he found himself patting the log

beside him, wiping the snow off with his glove as he did so.

"It's okay," he said. "You'll figure something out."

He'd figure something out, too.

She stayed standing with her arms crossed over her chest. Her gaze moved from the fire to the trees and then the dark skies above. "I can't stop thinking about the stuff Bud said."

He almost laughed. Iris was the most stubborn person he'd ever met, in all the best ways. When she grabbed hold of something, she never let it go until she'd worried it to death.

"What stuff?" he asked. "You mean, that he called you naive and foolish?" She nodded. "But why? Those four months we spent hanging out together, I heard people call you way worse. I mean, I've practically heard you called every bad name in the book. It took a whole lot of self-control not to grab each and every one by the scruff of the neck and make them apologize to you. But I followed your lead, and you always rolled with it."

Her gaze fell on his face, and he wondered if he'd ever be able to look at her without feeling something catch in his chest.

"Because maybe what Bud said is true," she said. "Maybe I am naive. And foolish. Because I really cared about you. Like a lot."

She walked over to the far side of the firepit, cleared off a log and sat. The fire danced between them. She rested her elbows on her knees and looked at him through the flames.

"Your friendship meant everything to me, Mack," she said. "You were my favorite person on the planet. I spent more time with you than anyone. And you fooled me. And if I'm not able to see when someone I'm that close to is tricking me, then maybe Bud's right and I really am foolish and naive."

"Don't." He stood suddenly, even as he felt his phone ringing again in his pocket, demanding his attention. "Just stop it with all that. It hurts me to see you sitting there beating yourself up, and it hurts even worse to know it's because of me."

She looked up at him, her words seemingly frozen on her tongue.

"First of all," he said, "I'm really, really good at what I do. I'm a professional actor, I guess you'd say. I step into a new life, take on a new persona and pretend it's who I am. It's what I do and it's what I've done for a very long time. Even before I became a cop, I had a lot of practice at editing myself and pretending to be who my father wanted me to be. So, there's that."

Her chin quivered slightly, and then it rose.

"Second," he said, "I've never lied to you. I was really vague about some details. But I never actually lied to you—"

"So you really do know what it's like to go to bed hungry?" she asked.

Oh, why did she have to choose now of all moments to jump in, and that of all questions to ask him?

"Yes, I did." *But not for the reasons you thought.*

"And you really did come home to find your dad

had stolen every cent you earned at your part-time job and sold your car?"

"Yes." *But not in the way you'd expect.*

"And you really were beaten up and punched by school bullies?"

"Yes, I really was," Mack cut her off. "And most important, I really did want you to get to know me—the real me. As much of me as I could show you safely, and then more than that. There is absolutely nothing wrong with you, Iris. It's just that there's a whole lot wrong with the world. But you don't focus on the bad stuff. You're like someone who walks into a junkyard and only sees the perfectly restored classic hiding inside the wreck. You see who people could be. And that's not foolish. That's special. That's worth everything. Because most people never have anyone who looked at them the way you do. Ever. I know I never did."

And it hurt more than she'd probably believe to know she'd never look at him like that again.

His phone was ringing persistently. Whatever Liam wanted, he wasn't about to wait a moment longer. Mack pulled out his phone, glanced at the screen and then up at Iris. The reception was weak and he needed higher ground.

"I've got to take a phone call," he said, "and that means I need a few minutes of privacy. But I don't want you to have to leave the fire and go back into the cold camper. So I'm going to walk up the hill, just far enough that you won't overhear me, but where I can get a stronger signal and still look down and keep an eye on you. Is that okay?"

"Yeah." She nodded and stretched out her hand for the water bottle. He handed it back to her. "I'll be here. I'm not going anywhere."

"Okay," he said. There wasn't anywhere really for her to go. "I won't be long." He put the phone to his ear as he walked away and pressed the button.

"Hello, Mack here," he said. "I'm sorry. I needed a minute. I was dealing with something important."

"Understood," Liam said, and everything in his voice implied he just wished they'd spoken sooner. "Are you alone?"

He glanced over his shoulder at where Iris sat beside the fire. "I will be," he said. "One moment. I'm going to try to get a better signal. Also, to warn you, the phone wasn't charging, so it might cut out on us. Fortunately, Iris has a phone as well and there should be a charger in the camper."

He walked up the hill, looking back over his shoulder every few moments at the soft glowing light of the campfire. "What's going on?" he asked.

"I'll start with the good," Liam said, "and then move on to the bad when you're confident you can't be overheard."

"Okay."

"Local RCMP raided Crow's Farm ten minutes ago," Liam said. "They got on it fast. Huge operation. They made eighteen arrests, including Corvus and Eddie, and are now securing the facility."

Mack sent a prayer of thanksgiving to the dark skies above.

"Yeah," Liam said. "The local guys are loving us

right now. Also, Seth said to let you know he's now eighteen percent through Iris's map and so far only about a quarter of the data is bad news."

"Okay. And what's the problem?"

"Oscar Underwood has been granted bail," Liam said. "He's being released in a few hours."

"What?" Mack glanced down the hill; Iris had turned toward his shout. He gritted his teeth and strode faster. "How? Why?"

"They reduced the charges," Liam said. "No more kidnapping. No more forcible confinement or threats of violence. He's now just being charged with a bunch of labor violations."

Mack let out a long breath like someone had just knocked the wind from his lungs. He leaned back against a tree and looked up at the sky. "How can they do that? Iris already has Underwood's Jackals after her! They destroyed her homeless center. Just think of how much more of a threat Underwood will be to her life outside of prison, especially with the resources at his disposal."

"Well, she's the one who ran from witness protection and won't let you take her in," Liam said. "Maybe the fact prosecutors knew she'd disappeared had something to do with their decision."

It was something Mack himself would have probably said, if he'd been on the other side of the conversation. But still Mack felt something shoot through him, hot, protective and fierce. "You are not going to blame Iris for this."

"Whoa, I didn't say I was blaming her," Liam said.

"Personally, I don't blame her one bit for not wanting to return to witness protection after what happened. I'll be the first to admit that if I was in her shoes, I'd try to strike out on my own. I was just dropping a hypothesis. You and I also both know that local Toronto police were turning a blind eye to Underwood for months. Maybe he was bribing them and still is. I don't know, and neither do you." He sighed loudly. "But you know the way this works. The best way to get that man behind bars where he belongs is to get Iris to fully cooperate with police, and that means getting her back within witness protection."

"I know." Mack closed his eyes. Even if he and Iris testified to the Jackal attack earlier that evening at the diner—which now felt like years ago—unless they caught the men and proved Underwood hired them, they had nothing.

But how would he explain all this to Iris?

"Jess and I are going to head up to your location by helicopter," Liam added. "There's an extreme cold weather alert hitting tonight. We still need some time to sort things at our end and then the flight's a few hours, but we should be there before five in the morning."

"Thank you," Mack said. He just prayed he'd convince Iris to return to witness protection by then. "The picture of the map I sent Seth had photos from the homeless center taped around it. Some of those people were found in the Oscar Underwood raids, but others weren't, and Iris is extremely worried about those that are still missing. They're also firsthand witnesses to who the Jackals are and what they did. Maybe Seth can find them."

"It's worth a try," Liam said. "Look, I know you're in a difficult situation. But we're all behind you and we're all praying for you."

An engine sounded in the night. Mack turned and ran toward the campfire. *No, no, it can't be!* The truck's headlights were on. It was leaving, pulling the camper behind it.

"She's running!" he shouted.

"You're kidding!" Liam exclaimed.

"No!" Mack pelted through the snowy trees down the hill so fast he nearly tripped, watching helplessly as the camper's taillights disappeared into the trees. "She left me." He gasped a breath and looked around the campsite. The empty water bottle lay on the ground by his feet. "She took off and left me here. She's gone."

"Hands on the wheel," said the slender, red-masked Jackal as he held a knife to her throat. "Nice and steady."

She gritted her teeth and prayed for help, trying to block out the sharp prick of the blade against her skin. The Jackal's face mask was even more crude up close, with a grotesque painted mouth full of jagged teeth. It had been the knife to the throat that had kept her from screaming.

She'd been walking back to the camper when he'd caught her, leaping out from the shadows and clasping one hand over her mouth while the other held the knife. Then he'd forced her into the vehicle and told her to drive.

Help me, Lord! Please help Mack find and rescue me!

She didn't know what hurt worse, the knife at her throat, the fear in her chest or the fact Mack probably thought she'd just run off.

But he would know she hadn't left him, right? He had to know she was in trouble and there was no way she'd just take the truck and run, despite the fact they'd been firing words back and forth at each other ever since escaping Crow's Farm. They hadn't been fighting exactly. They'd been doing something else entirely that she couldn't quite understand.

"Where are you taking me?" she asked, keeping her voice low and measured.

The Jackal didn't answer. He had to have gotten there somehow, which meant he had a vehicle stashed somewhere and there was probably at least one more Jackal in the area. But for a moment there was nothing but the sound of the sides of the truck and camper scraping against tree branches. To her left, she could see the vast, empty blackness of the frozen lake spreading out between the trees.

Dear Lord, how can I alert Mack? How can I escape this?

"What do you want?" she asked. She scanned the figure beside her in the darkness, searching for any form of human connection with the man beneath the mask. He might not feel like giving her answers but being quiet was never one of her strong suits. "How did you even find me? Was there a tracker on the camper? Or on the truck? When was it installed? Or did an actual person tip you off? Who?"

He shifted in his seat, like even the sound of her voice irritated him. The knife blade moved away from her skin for just a second before she could feel the cold of it brushing against her throat again.

"You really need to learn to mind your own business," he said, "and to keep your mouth shut."

Well, he might have kidnapped her, but she'd apparently struck a nerve. She wondered why.

"Don't see that happening," Iris said. If her voice rattled him, then she was going to keep talking. Back when Mack had volunteered at the homeless center, she'd heard him tell the youth that their voice was one of the strongest weapons they had. And she would use hers for all she was worth. Now what else could she do? He had a knife. She had a great big powerful truck.

"If you keep talking, I'll cut your throat," he said, and something wavered in his voice.

"You do that, and I'll crash the truck," she said. "So, I don't think so. Also, I'm pretty sure you want me alive. Because ever since I first ran into you guys a few hours ago, you've never tried to kill me."

She held her breath and waited a moment. Her heart pounded fearfully as she prayed her instincts were right.

Then slowly, he shifted, moving the knife over to the side of her throat.

Okay, so maybe that confirmed her hunch that he wanted her scared, silent and compliant, but not actually dead. She took as deep a breath as she could, calming her spirit and asking God for help. Then she turned back to the red-masked Jackal, and that's when she realized he wasn't wearing a seatbelt.

"Whatever's going on," she said, "and wherever Underwood wants you to take me, you don't have to do it. You can walk away and find a better path. It's not too late for you."

He swore under his breath, almost a snarl. "I'd shut up if I were you."

Yeah, but he wasn't her. "What do you really want?" she asked.

He didn't answer.

"Where are you taking me?" she pressed. "How did you find me?"

Still, no answer.

"I get it, Oscar Underwood wants me to disappear so that I don't testify at his trial," she said. "But I'm not the only person who knows about his crimes."

And she knew without a doubt that Mack would never stop seeking justice for her death.

"I said to shut up!" His voice thundered through the truck. The tip of the knife dropped to the top of her shoulder.

Help me, God! She yanked the wheel hard to her left. The tip of the knife sliced through her heavy coat, barely nicking her arm. The red-masked Jackal swore. But it was too late for him to do anything but hold on— the truck careened through the trees and down toward the frozen lake.

"Stop!" he shouted, sounding young and panicked. "Stop now!"

But she couldn't brake even if she wanted to. One way or another she was careening down toward the lake. She hit the hazard light button, and her four-ways started flashing in the night like a beacon. She leaned on the steering wheel until the horn blared.

Come on, Mack, hear me! See me! Find me!

"Stop now!" the Jackal shouted. "Missy! Please!"

Missy?

"How do you know that name?" For a second, she froze. The only people who called her that were those who'd visited the homeless center. Was the Jackal one of her former street kids? Or did he know that name another way?

The truck went faster, jumping and rocking as the descent grew steeper.

"Missy!" he yelled. "You need to stop!"

There was something in his voice that made her think that whatever he meant, it was about far more than just a crashing truck.

"How do you know my nickname?" she shouted. "Who are you? Let me help you!"

He yanked the door open and a panicked shout filled the air as he tossed himself out. The door swung on its hinges.

Then the trees broke in front of her and for a moment she was airborne, nothing but empty air beneath her tires and the weight of the camper behind her like an anchor. Then truck and camper hit the ice, one after the other, and she skidded out across the frozen lake like a space shuttle breaking orbit with a parachute trying to drag it back. She spiraled helplessly, holding on and praying. Then she heard a crack and the nose of the truck pitched forward so suddenly she fell against the steering wheel.

The ice cracked beneath her.

EIGHT

Mack pelted through the trees toward the flashing lights as they blinked on and off like a beacon in the darkness, casting the crashed truck and frozen lake in an eerie sea of light for barely an instant before turning the scene dark before his eyes again.

What had she been thinking? Why had she driven off like that? Why had she shot out onto the ice? Even as the questions crossed his mind, his heart was pierced with the fear that she hadn't done it willingly. The horn had stopped blaring, leaving nothing but the eerie sound of cracking ice behind. He could see the cab of the truck sink deeper and deeper beneath the ice.

All Mack could do was run.

"Update?" Liam's voice came from Mack's breast pocket, and Mack realized he hadn't paused long enough to end the call. "What's going on?"

He yanked out the phone and shouted, "Iris is in danger! I'll call you back. Don't stop praying."

"Will do," Liam said firmly. "God be with you."

"You, too." Mack hung up the phone so quickly he

wasn't even sure if Liam had heard his answer. He couldn't afford to pause. Not for a moment, not for a second, not while Iris's life was in danger. He dashed down the snowy hill, through the trees and toward the ice.

"Iris!" He cupped his hands and shouted into the night. "Can you hear me?"

"Mack!" Her voice met his ears and his feet sped faster. "I'm here! I've climbed onto the truck and it's sinking!"

The hazard lights flashed, and he saw her slender figure crouched on the sharply slanting cab of the truck.

"Iris, hold on!" he shouted. "I'm coming!"

Then his feet hit the ice and he ran as fast as he could along the shoreline toward the flashing lights. The scene flickered from light to dark in front of him as the truck slid deeper and deeper into the lake, nose first and anchored only by the camper behind it. Iris climbed across the slanting cab toward the bed of the truck. He gasped for breath. As he watched, she jumped from the tilted bed onto the top of the camper and crouched there gingerly. The sinking truck pulled the camper closer to the water.

"Don't jump!" he shouted. "Wait for me! I'll catch you!"

If she jumped and hit a fissure, she could break through the ice and go under. But if she leaped toward him, he could brace himself, catch her and pull her to safety.

The ice groaned loudly under the camper's weight.

Mack's feet slid beneath him, and another crack split the air as more ice gave way.

"Just hold on!" he shouted. "I'm almost there!"

"Mack!" She screamed his name as if it were wrenched from her lungs. "Look out behind you!"

A tranquilizer dart brushed his shoulder, tearing the edge of his sleeve before falling ineffectively to his feet. Mack glanced back in time to see a snarling face.

The green-masked Jackal threw his huge bulk at him, and Mack hit the ice with the weight of the criminal on top of him. Desperately, Mack rolled over, blocking the Jackal's punches. A fist hit Mack's jaw and pain shot through him, stunning him just long enough for the Jackal to start fumbling for another tranquilizer dart.

Yeah, there was no way Mack was going to let him load it. He braced his palms behind him on the ice and kicked up with both feet, tossing the Jackal off so hard that he flew onto the ice. Mack leaped up and yanked his gun from his holster as the Jackal got to his feet and stumbled backward.

"On your knees!" Mack shouted. "Drop all weapons and place your hands on top of your head."

The Jackal hesitated. Mack got him securely in his sights and prayed he would surrender.

An engine roared somewhere in the trees, and headlights flashed. The Jackal turned and sprinted across the ice. Mack pulled the trigger. His gun misfired, and visceral pain spread through Mack's core as he watched the man disappear into the trees.

At this distance in the dark, it would take a precision shot to hit him and it would be almost impossible to guarantee he wouldn't hit something life threatening. Even grazing the man could lead to dangerous levels of bleeding, considering how far away they were from shelter or medical attention.

The Jackal had lurked outside Iris's home, left two bullets in Mack's chest and almost killed him. He'd somehow found Iris twice, both at the diner and again here. But with Iris's truck gone, and no guarantee anyone else was around to save a fallen comrade, Mack couldn't risk shooting the Jackal and letting him die. Chasing after him wasn't even an option.

Only one thing that mattered, and that was saving Iris.

He turned and ran toward her, throwing caution to the wind and pelting straight across the ice, even as it grew thinner and thinner under his feet. She was crouching lower on the camper now, like she was trying to find a way to climb down inside a window.

"Just stay there!" he shouted. "The ice is going to break!"

"But I need to get inside!" She grabbed the edge of the camper with one hand and leaned down. "I need to save my stuff!"

The truck's headlights flickered on and off eerily under the ice.

"You can't! It's going to go under and take you with it!"

She was only a few yards away. The ice cracked. The camper lurched, dropping several feet into the water. Iris screamed, clinging to the top of the camper as it nearly tossed her off into the water.

"Jump!" he yelled. He pelted forward. "Just jump, and I'll catch you!"

She flung herself through the air as he ran toward her. Her body hit his, knocking him off balance and tossing them both backward onto the ice. The air flew from his lungs, but his arms tightened around her, and he clutched her to his chest. She shuddered against him.

"It's okay," he whispered. "You're okay, Iris. I've got you."

But any response she gave was lost in the sound of the ice groaning beneath his back.

"Come on," Mack said. She felt him shift underneath her, then he crawled to his feet and reached for her hand. "The ice is going to break. We've got to go. Now."

She stumbled to her feet and looked back. The camper was bobbing in the water now, the air inside keeping it afloat as water seeped in. Desperation welled up inside her. She couldn't lose her camper. Every last thing she owned was inside. If it sank, she'd have nothing.

"No!" She took a step toward the camper, but Mack's hand tightened on hers, pulling her back. She watched helplessly as everything she owned sank deeper and deeper beneath the water.

She couldn't just stand here and watch everything she owned disappear. She had to save something—her wallet, her phone, her Bible, her gun, the little box of cash that now served as her bank account, the emergency backpack she kept ready in case she ever had to grab what she could and flee. But all that was gone, sinking beneath the water.

"I can't lose everything!" She wrenched her hand away from Mack and turned toward the water. "I have to save something! I have to try!"

She felt his hands land softly but firmly on her shoulders.

"I'm not going to pick you up and drag you back to shore." His voice was deep and warm in her ear. "If you want me to let you go, I will. I'll stand right here on the ice watching and waiting, ready to try to rescue you the moment you scream for help or start to drown. But you won't make it. The water's too cold, and you won't be able to swim. The cracks in the ice will spread and soon the space we're standing on will be under water. So, please, come with me, get off the ice, don't risk your life over things that can be replaced."

But they weren't just some things, they were all of her things. Everything she had left to her name. She'd never had that much to begin with, but then she'd packed up everything she owned and emptied her bank account to buy the camper and truck.

A sob escaped her lips as she watched the camper sink. He was right, she knew it, but just how much was taking down Oscar Underwood going to cost her? Just how much was she going to lose?

Mack tugged her shoulder gently, just enough to let her know that he was there. She turned toward him, and her eyes met his in the dying flashes of the submerged taillights. Anguish filled his gaze and she remembered that the ice was at risk of cracking underneath his feet every much as it was beneath hers.

"I'm so sorry," he said softly. "But we have to go."

Hot tears rushed to the corners of her eyes. The groaning of the ice grew louder. Any moment now, the lake would split beneath them and drag them under. She looked back. Only the top of the camper remained now. The world grew darker as the lights disappeared deeper and deeper under the lake. Mack was right; it was all gone and he would let himself drown before he ran and left her there.

She slid her right hand into his. "I know."

He didn't say anything. He just took her hand. They ran together across the lake and back toward the shore. Ice splintered behind them, like distant thunder cracking the sky.

Then she felt snow under her feet again. They pressed on until dense rocks and trees sprung up around them. Only then, when she was certain they were on solid ground, did they stop and turn back, toward the empty hole in the ice where every last cent, every last scrap she'd once owned was now lost.

"He called me Missy," she said. "The red-masked Jackal called me Missy while he was holding a knife to my throat. My homeless center is gone, my life is known and now criminals know my nickname. What if he was someone who visited the homeless center?"

"Iris," Mack said. "I'm so sorry. I would do absolutely anything in my power to fix this for you."

"I know." She turned toward him again and could

barely see his face in his darkness. "If you could save me from all this, you would."

"Yeah." He dropped her fingers, but then he reached for her with both hands, letting them rest gently just above her hips, as if holding her in place, neither pulling her close or pushing her away. "And I know this is the worst possible time to tell you this, but I don't think waiting is going to make it any easier. The reason Liam was calling was to let me know that some of the charges have been dropped against Oscar Underwood, and they're letting him out on bail pending trial."

Frustration shot through her, balling her hands into fists. How was this even happening? How had everything been stripped away from her—family, friends, her job, the homeless center she'd created and now everything she'd owned—in order to take down this criminal and still lose?

Lord, I sacrificed everything to stop Underwood, because people were in danger and I believed it was what You wanted me to do. And now it's all gone.

"Go ahead and scream, or cry, or hit me if you need to," Mack said. "Whatever it takes right now. Because I care about you, I'm here for you, and no matter what, I'm not leaving you alone in this."

Suddenly as she heard him say those words, something broke inside her, like she'd been holding back a dam and now a wave of emotion was crashing over her. Tears of anger, fear and pain coursed from her eyes and she found herself tumbling forward into his arms. He caught her there and held her, safe and warm against his chest.

After a long moment her tears stopped, but still he held her. His hand brushed her head and then fingers stroked the back of her neck.

"I just wish I could undo all this," he said. "I wish none of this had ever happened, and that I'd found a way to take Oscar and the Jackals down without ever involving you."

She tilted her face toward him. "Don't say that," she said. "Because I'm always going to be thankful you came into my life."

He gasped and she felt his breath brush her face. "How can you say that? Anyone in your shoes would wish they'd never met me."

"But I'm not anyone," Iris said. "Mack? You infuriate me. You've hurt me. And when I heard that you were dead, it felt like someone reached inside my heart and tore off a piece of it. But that doesn't mean I'm not thankful for the amazing, unexpected friendship we had. I never experienced anything even close to what we had with anyone else." Her shoulders rose and fell. "And maybe I won't ever again."

"I don't get how you can say that," he began.

She reached up and brushed a hand along his beard and his words fell silent. "That's because you don't get how much I really, really liked you," she said.

"I really, really liked you, too, Iris."

She felt his touch grow firmer on the back of her neck. She leaned forward and their lips met.

Their kiss was gentle and tentative at first, as if he wasn't quite sure she was really there. Then it deepened, with a confidence that made her know somehow, deep inside, that in all those months they'd spent together as friends, Mack had thought about kissing her just about as many times as she'd thought about kissing him.

When they broke the kiss, they hugged each other even tighter, and it felt like coming home to a place she'd been homesick for her whole life.

He let her go, she peeled her arms away from him, and he stepped back. Silence settled between them that neither of them seemed ready to break.

His phone beeped. He stumbled two steps away, like a man waking up from a dream, and glanced at it. He frowned, his face illuminated in the glow of the screen. "We've got a new problem."

"Your team is calling," she said.

"No." He blew out a long breath. "That's the signal to let me know my battery is low. I thought it was good, but it apparently hasn't been charging properly since it was dropped in the snow."

He glanced up at the hill ahead of them, thick with trees, and then back toward the lake.

"Unfortunately, any phone charging option is now in the lake," he said. "We're in the middle of nowhere with no vehicle and a phone that's down to just ten minutes of juice."

NINE

Ten minutes. The words seemed to echo in the dark woods around them. She had nothing—no plan, no vehicle, no money and nothing but the clothes on her back. It was freezing cold, they were up to their knees in snow in the middle of nowhere, and now, Mack had told her they were ten minutes away from losing their only contact with the outside world.

She closed her eyes and prayed.

Lord, I am so lost, I don't even know what to do.

The deep murmur of Mack's voice made her open her eyes. His phone was to his ear, and he was talking to someone quickly. "Yup… Got it… Will do… Talk to you then… You, too."

He ended the call, turned off the phone and with it their final remaining sliver of light. With the light of the truck and camper now gone, pinpricks of starlight spread out above her.

"So, here's the deal," Mack said. "Seth doesn't know how the Jackals found us. Liam and Jess are on their way to meet up with us, but that will take hours and we need to keep moving. Both in case the Jackals come back and also because it's only going to get colder. Seth's identified a motel about a forty-minute walk from here. The route is mostly back roads, which he thinks should reduce the risk of being spotted by drivers. We'll walk along the tree line. Seth and I have agreed that I'll turn on my phone every fifteen minutes, so he can map where we are on the GPS. It's almost one thirty in the morning now. Liam and Jess hope to reach us by five."

So, in four and a half hours then. And then what would happen? She had nothing left. In the past few hours since spotting Mack in the diner, even the false sense of hope, safety and direction that had kept her going for so long had been taken from her. She had no choice but to go into witness protection now.

"Also," Mack added, "I'm down to two bullets with no way to reload for now. But don't worry. It'll all be fine."

Fine. The word rolled around in her head as they walked. It wasn't *good*, but *fine* was all she had left.

They trudged onward and upward through the trees until they hit a road. They followed it, sticking close to the tree line and dropping flat to the ground whenever they heard a vehicle approaching. They walked in near silence, barely even making small talk. Despite the brief and spontaneous moment of closeness, now things were awkward again, as if neither of them knew what to say.

She wondered if he regretted kissing her. Maybe. But she didn't. Yes, it had been foolish, sudden and unexpected. They'd be saying goodbye in a matter of hours. She'd go into witness protection and Mack would be disappearing out of her life into another undercover assignment, and she'd try to rebuild her life somewhere. Yet, she didn't regret the fact she'd let herself, for one fleeting moment, show this strange, strong, complicated man how she felt about him.

Did she really have no choice but to go back into witness protection? Was she right to trust Mack? Could she trust his team that this time she'd be safe and the Jackals wouldn't find her? And who was she now without the homeless center? Her work had always been her calling and one she was deeply devoted to. Who did God want her to be now? What future did she have?

And how was she ever going to handle saying goodbye to Mack again?

Eventually they saw the dim, yellow lights of Noel's Motel off the highway. It was a low, squat building with only the sad, flickering light in the front office to show it was even open.

The man who greeted them from behind the counter was Noel himself, according to his nametag. Noel's tired eyes were locked on a television screen that showed the weather forecasts and rolling headline ticker of a twenty-four-hour news channel. Mack asked for adjoining rooms, preferably something with a living room if they had it. Noel shrugged and offered them two old-fashioned room keys attached to large plastic spoons, which she imagined was to keep people from losing them. Mack bought a bag full of overpriced toiletries and snacks from the two crowded shelves beside the front desk, along with every one of the cheap, knock-off phone chargers Noel had, to ensure the best probability of finding one that actually worked. Unfortunately, Noel didn't sell burner phones.

The stairs up to the second floor were outdoors. They were icy and slippery with puddles of gray slush.

Mack opened the door to the first suite, signaled for her to stay back while he did a sweep and then ushered her inside. The room had wood-paneled walls, a ceiling marked with water stains and a carpet in various shades of orange and brown. A small table, two folding chairs, a couch with one mismatched cushion and a single bed made up the rest of the room.

"Liam and Jess will meet us here," Mack said. He unlocked the door between the two rooms on her side. "I'm going to head next door. Leave the outside door locked, and I'll come back through this adjoining door. You should eat something and try to get some sleep if you can. I'm going to stay awake, pray and hope I can get one of these charging cables to give me juice for my phone. Don't worry. It won't be long until we're rescued."

He stepped forward, like he was thinking of hugging her, and then he stepped back again.

She waited until he left, then she locked the outside door behind her, sat down and took off her boots. She simply unzipped her coat and stuffed her hat and gloves into her pocket. It might be just after two o'clock in the morning and her entire body ached, but if Mack wasn't going to sleep, neither was she.

She opened the closest can of pop, took a swig and

then started on a bag of chips. She flipped the television on and watched as it crackled to life. The same news channel that had been showing in the office downstairs appeared on the screen in a hodgepodge of colors and words. It took her a few moments of clicking to realize it was the only channel not showing static, unless she wanted to input a credit card. She gave up and watched the feed scroll past without really looking. A high school student had won a national music competition, a charity knitting event was coming up for women's national health and there was a breaking news alert that a man had been shot and killed outside a building in Toronto with the promise of details to come. The temperature was expected to drop even further with a severe cold weather alert in effect. Someone in New Brunswick had turned themselves in after a stabbing outside a pizza place.

She heard the sound of Mack unlocking the door between their two suites.

"All clear." He stuck his head through. "You good in here?"

She nodded. "Yeah."

He popped back into his suite, leaving the door between their rooms open. She drained the pop and tossed the empty can in the garbage can. It bounced off the rim but fell in.

The television told her a new book on trains was coming out and that Toronto's mayor, Lisa Kats, was receiving the Order of Canada from the prime minister himself for her youth scholarship and charity work.

Iris closed her eyes. The days she'd protested outside

Mayor Kats's office, trying to get someone to listen to her about Oscar Underwood, seemed so very long ago. Iris wasn't sure the mayor deserved the praise she'd got in the past, let alone on this national stage. She especially objected to the fact the mayor threw lavish parties on her yachts for fashionable charitable causes and only gave her scholarships to high-achieving young people who went to private schools, instead of caring for the kind of people Iris saw walking through her door.

But now she just prayed that one day she'd be able to meet with Mayor Kats about reopening the homeless center. She asked God to help soften her own heart and be less stubborn about believing her own plans and vision were the right ones.

She heard the sound of water running from the other room, then the faint tap of something hitting porcelain, and it took her a moment to realize what it was. Mack was shaving. She vaguely remembered seeing him grab a pack of razors, a can of shaving cream and a small pair of scissors.

Her first witness protection handler had taken her to a motel that hadn't been much better than this one. Iris had lived there for three days, listening to a stranger give her the rules of living a life without friends or real connections with people. Then she'd moved to a small house on the edges of Hamilton, and her witness protection handler had become nothing more than a voice on a telephone she'd needed to talk to once a week and a name on a screen she had to text at predetermined times.

It was a life with no real relationships, no community and no home, knowing each conversation she had and each person she met could potentially risk her life. Being on the road hadn't been much better.

Was that what life had been like for Mack all those times he went undercover as Graves, or someone similar? Never really letting anyone get to know him? Having no real relationships with anyone at all? Was the friendship they shared really something just as rare and special to him as it had been to her?

"What are you watching?" Mack's voice drew her attention back to the room.

She opened her eyes. "It's the only channel I could get," she said.

Her voice trailed off as she turned to face him. Mack stood in the doorway, running a towel over his face. Then he pulled the towel away and suddenly she could see his beardless face.

There he was—the lines of his jaw, his cheeks, his grin—looking like the man she'd gotten so close to back in Toronto. The man she'd cared for and liked more than anyone she'd ever met.

Mack was back. The Mack she'd cared about. The Mack who'd meant the world to her.

She wanted to throw her arms around him and hug him. She also wanted to demand answers. How could he have gotten so close to her while undercover? Had he kissed her knowing his team was already on the way and they were about to leave each other's lives in mere hours? What happened now?

His keen blue eyes darted from her face to the screen. His gaze sharpened.

"What are you watching?" An edge moved through his voice so tense it was almost sharp.

"I told you, it's whatever news channel this place gets—"

"Turn it up! Now!"

She glanced around for the remote. He found it before she could and stepped between her and the television, momentarily blocking her view. She glanced past him. The news story about the murder in Toronto was on. White letters on a thick red bar read Manhunt.

"How long has this been on?" He pushed a button repeatedly and the volume grew louder.

"…Police have apprehended Hank Barrie of Sudbury in connection to the murder. Sources say Barrie was waiting for the victim inside a parking garage," an unseen female newsreader was saying.

"This story," Mack went on. "How long has it been airing?"

"I don't know," Iris said. "They've been teasing it ever since I came in. It's been appearing in the news scroll. But I don't know anything about it."

"A national warrant has been issued for RCMP Detective Mack Gray, who is accused of hiring Barrie to commit the murder…"

Her heart froze.

"Help me, Lord," Mack prayed under his breath.

She glanced past him at the screen. It was Mack, but as a much younger man, in a suit jacket and tie, with a thinner face and a leaner, almost hungry look to him, like an unfed wolf.

"Born Mackenzie Gravenhurst, only child of millionaires Patrick and Annie Gravenhurst, he was raised in a life of extreme wealth and privilege…"

"It's me." Mack turned to look at her. His face so pale, it echoed the unhealthy hue of the face on the screen.

"Mackenzie Gravenhurst is one of your aliases," she said. "Your covers?"

"No." His voice had a tinge of something like panic as he turned back to the screen. "I mean, that's actually me."

"But I don't understand," she began. "How is that you and who do they think you killed?" Instinctively she reached for his hand, her fingers brushing against his before he pulled away.

He raised his hand as if to shush her.

"…Confidential sources report that RCMP Detective Gray has been on probation pending inquiry into irregularities in his recent investigation of agricultural magnate Oscar Underwood," the voice on the television continued. "A national manhunt has been launched for Gray, who is accused of paying Barrie fifty thousand dollars cash to murder Underwood…"

Oscar's face filled the screen and Iris's heart dropped inside her chest like a broken elevator.

"Underwood was recently released on bail from jail where he'd been held in relation to alleged labor violations. Underwood was pronounced dead in hospital from a series of gunshot wounds to the chest and abdomen…"

He was dead? Oscar Underwood, the man she was testifying against, who'd plunged her life into chaos and sent his Jackal henchmen after her, was dead?

And Mack was accused of hiring the man who killed him?

"Gray is considered armed and dangerous. Anyone with information is asked to call 911…"

"We've got to go." Mack spun toward her. His eyes met hers. "Now."

Mack looked down at Iris sitting on the couch. His heart was smacking so hard against his chest he could barely breathe.

But her head was shaking.

"None of this makes any sense," she said. "Oscar can't be dead and you're not a millionaire. And who's Hank Barrie?"

The television switched to a story about a spelling bee. Mack hit the mute button.

"Barrie is a killer for hire, who'd sell out his own grandmother for enough money," Mack said. "Guaranteed he's banking on a very nice plea deal. Oscar Underwood could very much be dead, but someone is trying to frame me for it."

"But—but who's Mackenzie Gravenhurst…"

"He's me," Mack said, cutting her off before she said the words again. He shoved his feet into his boots, then scooped up hers and tossed them to her, before stooping to yank his laces tight. "I was born Mackenzie Gravenhurst, only child of millionaires Patrick and Annie Gravenhurst. My friends have always called me Mack and I legally changed my name when I was in the police academy. The fact that reporters figured out that I was born a Gravenhurst that fast is an interesting piece of the puzzle I have no time to even consider now. I'm guessing they were tipped off. But a millionaire cop accused of hiring a killer makes a pretty good news story."

He glanced out the window. The parking lot looked just as dark and empty as it had when they'd arrived. He checked that both the doorknob and deadbolt were locked, then dashed into the adjoining room and glanced at his phone. The screen was dead. His phone wouldn't charge and he had no way to contact his team.

Help me, Lord.

He threw his coat on. "Once Noel sees my face and figures out there's a national manhunt on for someone staying at his motel, he's going to call the police. So, we need to get out of here."

He stood up, crossed to the window and looked out at an alley below. They were only a single story off the ground, and the pavement was thick with snow. It wasn't great as far as landings went, but he could make it.

He ran back to Iris. She was still sitting on the couch, semi-frozen, with her foot halfway into her second boot. A myriad of expressions weaved across her face, from confusion to fear to disbelief. She was probably in a bit of shock from new information overload. He understood, but they didn't have time to waste.

"So even your entire childhood was a lie," she said slowly. "You really did lie to me about everything."

There was the faint crunch of a car pulling up outside. He crossed the floor and looked out. A lone cop car now sat on the far side of the lot. There were two officers inside.

"I didn't lie to you about any of it, I promise." He dropped to one knee in front of her and gently helped tie her laces. "I know it looks that way, and I don't have time to explain it to you now. When I can, I will. But right now, I need to run. I need to get somewhere safe, regroup, contact my team and figure it out from there."

He finished the laces of one boot and started on the other.

"There are already two cops outside," he said. "Pretty soon there will be more. And I'm not going to just turn myself in to the first cop I see and hope for the best. For all I know, they've been told to shoot me on sight. But even if all they do is throw me in jail for a while as this thing is being sorted out, I know a whole lot of convicted criminals who'd be all too happy to see the man who put them there tossed in with them. Discovering I'm actually both a cop and a millionaire's son is not going to make them any less hungry for revenge."

He could count on one hand the number of times he'd felt truly terrified of something and this was one of them. If he was tossed into general population, he'd be in a constant fight for his life.

"But I'm going to get us out of here," he said, taking her hands. "Here's the plan. I'm going to jump out the bathroom window into the alley behind the motel. Once I do, I want you to wait until you see me disappear around the end of the alley and then start screaming. I mean really screaming, full volume, enough that any law enforcement in this place will come running up here full speed to see what's wrong. While you're distracting them, I'll nab us transport. As soon as you hear them coming, run through to the adjoining room and lock yourself in. I'll be back outside the window waiting for you faster than they can break through all three doors. You jump out, I'll catch you, we'll run and regroup with witness protection." He got to his feet and stuffed the snacks he'd bought back into the plastic bag. Then he tucked the bag inside his coat. "Don't worry, I'll keep you safe."

"Safe from what?" Iris's hazel eyes met his. "If Oscar's dead, there's no witness protection for me anymore, right? Even if I wanted to be relocated, the RCMP isn't going to do it, because there's no trial for me to testify at, there's no big bad guy for the RCMP to protect me from now, and no reason for Oscar's Jackals to keep pursuing me. I'm not a witness anymore. I'm just a person who has nothing and whose life was ruined."

His heart stopped. How had he not seen this? What was he thinking? He couldn't ask Iris to come with him. He was about to run from the police because he'd been framed for murder and there was a warrant out for his arrest. That was his choice and he could make peace with it. But he couldn't just take a civilian along with him for the ride. Or ask this incredible woman to go on the run with him, just because his life was in danger.

"You're right," he said, the words tumbling from his mouth. "If Oscar's dead, you're not a witness anymore. Your life might no longer be in danger. I don't know for sure. You could walk right up to the police outside, and they'll probably help you. There's a lot I don't know right now. But I do know I can't ask you to come with me. I can't guarantee that's the right decision or tell you that's what you should do."

"I know." She stood and faced him. "Believe me, after what I've just learned about you, part of me is tempted to just say goodbye right now, let you run and try to make it on my own. After I go talk to the police and confirm Oscar's really dead, I'll just lie low for a while until I'm sure the Jackals are no longer after me and then somehow get home to my family and start my life over again. I've made it just fine so long on my own, you're wanted by police and now Oscar's gone. But…"

The word hung in the air for a long moment, and she took a deep breath. Then she stepped toward him. Her hand brushed the side of his face and he felt himself shiver as her fingers touched his damp, freshly shaved skin.

"But there's something inside me that's just not ready to let you go," she said. "It's telling me I'm still in danger and that the safest place to be right now is by your side. So, whoever you've been and whatever you've done, do you give me your word right here and now that you will keep me safe?"

He nodded. "With my life."

A knock came on the door.

"Hey!" The voice was Noel's and uncertain. "Can you open up? Just checking in to see how you're finding things?"

She heard the fiddle of keys in the lock. Any second now, he'd realize she'd also locked the deadbolt.

"I know you will," she said. Her lips quickly darted over Mack's cheek. "And even though I don't know what to think right now, I'd rather trust my life with you than with anyone else. Now go!"

TEN

"**Y**ou're incredible," Mack said softly as he turned and dashed for the window. "When we get out of here—"

But she never heard how he was going to end the sentence. His words were swallowed up by more knocking on the door.

"Hello?" Noel called. "Are you there?"

Cold air brushed the back of her neck. She turned from the door. The window behind her was open and Mack was gone.

"Hello!" Noel's voice grew louder. "I need you to open the door."

And she needed to distract him long enough to enable Mack to sort their escape.

"Hey!" she called back. "I'm here. Just give me a minute. I was watching TV."

Silence fell. All right, she seemed to have bought herself a moment at least. She tiptoed to the door and looked through the peephole. Noel definitely looked worried. He was flanked by two male uniformed police officers, one on either side. Falling snow whipped sideways at them, flying in and out of the yellow light and the darkness beyond.

She walked backward across the room and looked out the opposite window, to where freshly falling snow had already begun to erase the line of footprints leading around the side of the building. Mack was gone. She breathed another prayer for his safety.

Then she turned again to the door. "Is everything okay?" she asked.

"Oh, oh yeah, everything's fine," Noel said.

"So, what is all this about?"

"Nothing," Noel lied. "Just checking in to see if you have enough towels and stuff."

She glanced through the peephole again.

Am I making the right decision, Lord? Should I just let Mack go and open the door?

"Who all's out there?" she asked. "What is this really about?"

As she watched, the police officer to Noel's right shook his head. Both cops pulled their weapons. Then Noel slid his hand over the peephole, blocking her view. Whatever they were going to do, they were going to do it now.

"Uh, no one," Noel said. The tone of his voice reminded her of every desperate, lying person she'd had to turn away from the homeless center's doors for trying to smuggle in weapons, drugs or alcohol. "Just me. All alone. Can you open the door now?"

No. Not for a man blatantly lying to her. A suspicion rose up the back of her spine that if they opened the door and found Mack gone, they'd arrest her for aiding and abetting him.

"I need to get dressed," she called.

And hopefully once she was done, her ride would be there.

She did up the zipper of her coat, pulled her hat down over her head and then silently walked into the adjoining room, locking both doors behind her. A crash sounded from the other room. The cops were done asking. They were breaking down the door.

She glanced from the door that led to the adjoining room to the door that led outside. How long until they broke through? And which door would they break through first? Then came another crash, loud and deafening, shaking the air like a detonation. Voices shouted from the room she'd left just moments ago.

"Police! Come out with your hands up!"

It was too late to change her mind. She shoved the window open and looked outside. A tall, white police SUV was parked just outside the window. Mack jumped out and ran around to her side, standing in the space between the vehicle and wall.

"Come on!" He reached up both arms toward her. "Time to go."

Iris didn't hesitate. She swung her legs through the window, sat on the ledge, took a deep breath, said a silent prayer and let her body drop. For a moment she tumbled through empty air. Then she landed against Mack's chest and his arms tightened around her.

"Gotcha," he said softly. He set her down on the snowy ground. "Now, let's get out of here."

"You stole a police car." *And I'm trusting you on that, just like I am on everything else.*

He didn't answer, just opened the passenger door for her. She slid inside and buckled her seat belt. He shut the door for her and ran around to the other side.

"Hey, welcome back. It's nice to see you again." Seth's voice came from her left.

"Seth!" She turned.

The hacker's face filled a small computer screen nestled within the complicated electronics system between the two front seats. She guessed Mack still hadn't gotten the phone working, so had found a way to call Seth using the police car's built-in computer.

"Live and in color." Seth beamed.

"Don't you ever sleep?" Iris asked.

"Less than you'd think."

Mack jumped into the driver's side, buckled his seat belt and pulled the car off the road and into the trees, keeping the headlights off.

"Have they noticed you're gone?" Seth asked.

Iris glanced behind her. "Not yet, I don't think. They might still be breaking through doors in the hotel room trying to find us."

Mack nodded. He pulled the car onto a small service road that ran barely more than a car's width behind the motel and gunned the engine. "Any idea who set me up for the murder of Oscar Underwood?" he asked.

"Not yet," Seth said and frowned. "And I am sorry. Because one criminal bribing another to do a bad thing and frame a good guy for it is the kind of transaction that usually leaves some kind of trail somewhere, even if it's just rumors on the dark web."

"How about what the news was saying about Oscar Underwood?" Iris asked.

"You mean is he actually dead?" Seth asked. "Yeah, that's irrefutable. It's not impossible to fake the death of a high-profile person in a hospital, but it's unbelievably difficult and takes a lot of work and coordination. In this case, I can't find a single indication that any part of his shooting, transporting him to hospital and being pronounced dead was faked. We have multiple eye witnesses at every step of the process. I know we might be looking for a bigger conspiracy, but I can say confidently it's not a faked death. Oscar Underwood was definitely murdered."

Iris let out a long breath and leaned back against the seat. "So, he's really dead," she said.

"Very," Seth said. "Now, I've scrambled the car's tracker, so it can't be traced electronically. But I can't do anything about anyone who actually spots and chases you in real life."

"Understood," Mack said. "I found an unused burner phone in the car, but it's locked."

"I'll see if I can access it," Seth said. "But it might take a while."

"Well, hopefully we won't need it," Mack said. "We should be back at my vehicle before too long."

"Hold on one second, Seth," Iris said. "Can I mute you for a moment?"

"Actually, how about you hang up and call back?" Seth said. "I need to coordinate with Liam and Jess and figure out a new pickup location. Also, I'm thirty-five percent through that other data project you've got me working on."

"What data project?" Iris asked.

Neither man answered.

"Call me as soon as you've got a location for us," Mack said and ended the call.

"Please tell me why stealing a cop car wasn't an unbelievably dumb move," Iris said, turning to Mack, "and why I should still trust you."

"Well," Mack said, blowing out a hard breath, "let's start with the fact I'm only borrowing it just long enough to reach my truck and will definitely ensure that it's returned to the RCMP. The fact the cops at the motel will have backup coming means I didn't leave anyone stranded. It matches hundreds of identical cop cars, which means there'll be a lot of false sightings and people will also be more likely to not even notice it, since seeing a police vehicle is an everyday occurrence. And of course, because my phone still isn't working and this way I can talk to Seth and coordinate with my team. But the main reason I'd always go for hot-wiring a cop car over a civilian's vehicle is so no civilian ever has to face the panic of losing their personal property. I know what that feels like."

"Because your car was stolen by your father when you were a teenager?" she asked, feeling the bite in her voice. "Like you had to hitchhike across the country to get home from camp because your father emptied your bank account? I don't care that you're rich, but I don't get why you made up those stories and then told them to me so many times."

Mack's jaw set. He glanced at the screen as if double-checking they'd really ended the call with Seth. Then he stared straight ahead at the windshield and something seemed to tighten in the air until it almost hurt to breathe.

"Why did you tell me you grew up poor?" she asked.

"Why did you tell me you grew up rich?"

He shot the words back so quickly it stunned her. How dare he ask her that right now? Especially when he knew the answer to that question and how she'd meant it.

"Every single member of your extended family is living near or just below the poverty line," Mack said. "No one owns their own house, except for your parents and they're still heavily mortgaged, even though they're in their seventies. You're the only one who has more than a high school education. You grew up in a family that lived paycheck to paycheck. You got food boxes from your church at Christmas and never had new clothes, as far as I know, until you were twenty-three. And yet I've heard you, over and over again, tell me that grew up blessed and rich, so much richer than so many other people—"

"Because, like I've said a million times, there's more than one way of being rich!"

"Right," he said. "And there's more than one way of being poor. There's being starved of love, acceptance and attention. There's not being allowed to be yourself and growing up in a world where positive reinforcement is so rare, you're starving for someone, anyone, to tell you that they notice you or think you're okay."

"You told me you literally went to bed hungry," she said.

"And I did," Mack said, "over and over again. Because even though my mom did the best she could, she never stood up to my father. And my dad is..." He floundered a moment as if trying to find the right word. "My dad is a jerk, Iris, who used to send me to bed hungry all the time for failing to meet his standards."

Her chest tightened around her heart, and she found herself wanting to reach her hand across the darkened vehicle to take his. Instead she twisted the edges of her scarf in her fingers and his hands stayed white-knuckle on the steering wheel.

"All the stories I told you about being bullied in school until I figured out how to fit in and become invisible were also true," he added. "I grew up going to private schools full of wealthy people, but they're just the same as everyone else. They have the same types of problems. They just try to solve them differently than the people you grew up with. And not always in better ways. Sometimes worse. My dad really did take my car when I was sixteen and sell it, as punishment for some imagined offense I don't even remember. He really did empty my bank account when I told him I was leaving the really strict military-style summer camp he sent me to and I really did try to hitchhike across the country to get home. I have never asked my father for anything in my entire life. Not a single favor and not a single cent. And I never will."

He took a deep breath and Iris found herself both wanting to do something to help the boy he'd once been and praying for the man he was now.

"But how exactly do I explain a life like that to people like those in the homeless center?" he asked. "I'm asking that for real. When I was talking to all those kids who'd lost everything, how was I supposed to tell them that I'd grown up unbelievably rich, yet in a world where everything was uncomfortable, nothing was ever really mine and I had to pretend to be someone else to survive?"

He ran his hand over his head, and his voice dropped.

"How could I ever explain that to you?" he asked. "I'm embarrassed by it. It cuts me off from people and keeps them from seeing the truth about who I am and what I've lived. We met while you were camped outside Mayor Lisa Kats's office. What would you have thought if I'd strode up there and told you that I was the son of a millionaire, not a laid-off dishwasher? What if I'd shown up to volunteer at your homeless center as the man who was born Mackenzie Gravenhurst, the estranged son of a very wealthy couple who might or might not bequeath me millions depending on what mood my father was in when he wrote their wills? How could I have a real relationship with anyone who knew that?"

"I don't know," she said. "I really don't. I can't relate to anything you've been through. So I can't say how I'd handle it. I want to tell you that it wouldn't have made any difference to our friendship, but in reality I have no way to know how I would've reacted." She took a deep breath and held it a long moment. There was one story she hadn't had the courage to ask him about yet, and it was the one she wanted to know the truth of most of all.

"I heard you tell some people at the homeless center that you'd never had a girlfriend," she said. "Not for real and not in a way that mattered. Because the only time you ever caught feelings for someone, you never got up the courage to do anything about it because they were so rich and you were so poor."

He didn't even hesitate.

"Yeah," Mack said. "That was you, Iris. Even back then, I had major feelings for you."

I had major feelings for you. Had he really just said that? Blurting the words out to her like a teenager?

He'd never said anything like that to a woman before. Not even close. After a lifetime of not letting anyone in, Iris had gotten the closest that anyone ever had to seeing the man he was inside. And once he'd opened up his heart to her, he'd never quite been the same.

She still hadn't said anything, and he kept driving, hearing the winter wind blowing around them. He pulled onto a main road and turned the headlights on. They were far enough away from the motel that he'd look more suspicious driving with his lights off. He didn't dare glance at Iris, the beautiful, inspiring and challenging woman he still had feelings for and was on the cusp of losing again. How could he risk looking into her eyes when he knew she deserved so much better than a man like him?

"I could've wrapped up my undercover assignment with you in a couple of hours a day," he admitted. Now that he'd cracked his heart open, he might as well tell her everything. "That was what I thought the assignment would be, just hanging around during community meals and drop-in activities, and trying to gather intel. Instead, there was just something about you, Iris. I found myself staying late to clean up and coming in early and finding every possible excuse to see you both inside and outside of the center."

He swallowed hard. "I was put on probation after the shooting because there were concerns that maybe my cover had been blown because I'd gotten too close to you emotionally. I'd violated orders by confronting and chasing down the green-masked Jackal. That led to my superior officers discovering just how much time I'd been spending with you and that I'd admitted to Liam that I thought I was catching feelings for you—which I definitely was."

His eyes rose to the dark sky ahead. *Lord, I feel like I've messed everything up. I don't know what's going on or what to do. I just know that I want Iris to be safe and happy.*

He wasn't sure why it had taken him until now to even admit it to himself. But the fact he cared about her in a way he'd never cared for anyone else ever before was undeniable. He knew that right here and right now, in this car, speeding through the frozen dark, he'd been the most real and honest he'd ever been in his life. No matter how long he lived or what happened next, he'd never regret having gotten up the courage to tell her that.

Then he felt her hand brush his arm and slowly tug it toward her across the crowded front seat. Her fingers slid down his arm to his hand and linked through his fingers.

"Well, I had serious feelings for you, too," she said. "You were the first person I ever really wanted to be more than friends with and thought I could be."

Something swelled inside him, like a deflated hot air balloon filling with fresh air or an orchestra springing to life. His eyes met hers in the darkened vehicle, he saw the nervous smile on her lips, and he realized what this feeling was that he'd never felt before.

Hope.

"I can forgive a lot," Iris said, "and I can understand, some, that you were walking this tightrope of trying to let me in without telling me too much. But that was then and this is now. Just promise me that you'll never hide anything from me ever again."

"I—"

The screen began to ring. Seth must have found a location to meet up with his team and was back. Mack reached forward with their linked hands and pressed the button. Seth glanced down at their hands and his eyebrows rose.

"Uh, hey," Seth said. "I've got good, good and good news. Liam and Jess are less than three hours away, and I've found a really solid safe house. It's actually from the data I was analyzing, which is almost sixty percent done. As for the locked burner phone, I've located the serial number and have a plan to call it remotely, but it might take time. Although, so far, the photographic evidence you asked me to analyze—"

"One second!" Mack dropped Iris's hand and raised a finger. "I'm really, really sorry, Seth. But there's one thing I need to tell Iris."

Something he should've told her hours ago. Something he didn't want to tell her, because he never wanted to see that light dim in her eyes, but she deserved to know.

Seth raised his hands. "Okay, I'll be here."

"Thanks." Mack ended the call again. He debated whether or not to pull over for a moment, before he decided they'd be safest if he kept driving. Iris was still looking at him, worry and compassion washed across her face. He groaned.

God, I don't want to tell her about the map. I really don't. I don't want her to know I've been keeping her map from her, even if I did it for really good reasons.

And it hit him that he didn't have to tell her. He could choose not to and somehow hand-wave the whole problem away. If he wanted to, he'd be able to find a way to keep Iris from ever finding out.

And yet, wasn't that the whole point, that Iris was worth so very much more than that?

"I have to tell you something," Mack said. "Before I wiped your map of safe places clean, I took a quick picture of it and sent it to Seth."

Her jaw dropped.

"That secret project he's been working on has been analyzing the locations on your map to see which ones are safe and which ones aren't," he went on. "I told myself that I was doing it to protect you and that I would tell you in a few hours. I told myself that you'd be safer if I waited and gave you an edited list once Seth had removed all the places that could get you killed."

"You had my map." Iris said the words slowly, as if struggling to digest each one.

"I did," Mack said, "and I always planned to tell you. I just kept putting it off, after all it's only been a few hours and we've barely had time to breathe. I spent the last few hours trying to convince myself that waiting just a little while longer to tell you would be okay. But I was wrong. And I'm sorry."

Her face paled, she shook her head, and for a long moment she didn't say anything, as if her mind couldn't even find words.

"You...you betrayed me," she said. "You knew that as long as I didn't have it, you had a better chance of talking me into going back into witness protection."

Betrayal. Not a word that had ever crossed his mind when it came to this, but he couldn't deny it.

"You're right," Mack said. It hurt to think, it hurt to breathe, it felt like he was driving a sword deeper and deeper into his chest. "I didn't want you to run away on your own and get into trouble. I wanted to protect you. I wanted to keep you safe."

She closed her eyes. Silent words moved on her lips.

"I don't even know why I'm shocked," she said. "Let alone disappointed. This is exactly who you've always been. I'm the one who's foolish enough to keep trusting you. I'm the one who keeps choosing to listen and

believe you, over and over again. Why did I even jump
out of a window and run away with you? Why did I
decide to climb a wall to make sure criminals didn't
kill you? A criminal just told me that I was foolish and
naive. And here I am just a few hours later, holding
your hand and admitting I had feelings for you, without it even crossing my mind you'd keep something
like this from me."

His eyes met hers for a fleeting moment, wondering
if she could see the pain and regret bubbling up inside
him just as clearly as he could see hers. He needed to
fix this. He needed to fix this now.

"One second," he said. "Okay? Just give me one
second. Please."

She nodded, without knowing why he was asking
her to wait or what she was waiting for. And something
about the simple fact that even now she was trusting
him made the pain in his chest cut even more.

He called Seth.

"Hey." Seth looked up.

"You know that thing you do when you set up a
cell phone remotely?" Mack asked. "Where you prep
everything that should be on the cell phone, and then
somebody else takes an empty cell phone and con-
nects to the internet, and somehow it has all that information on it?"

Seth half shrugged. "Absolutely. Same way cell
phone repair places transfer your data onto a server
and then download it onto a new phone." He flashed a
quick half smile. "Only I do it better."

Was Mack really about to ask this? "Okay," he said,

"I should reach my vehicle in a little under an hour, barring any unforeseen interruptions. I have a new, unused cell phone in my bag of tricks. I want you to set it up for me remotely."

"Easily done," Seth said. "I take it you still can't get your phone working?"

"Yeah," Mack said. "But this one's not for me. It's for Iris. I need you to upload a copy of her map onto it, both the original picture and any enhancements you've done. And all the supplemental data you've been able to find out so far about the people and locations listed. Tabulate it somehow so that when she looks at a location, she'll immediately know everything she needs to know before she runs there."

"Okay…" Seth said. "It'll take some time, but that's doable."

Well, it was just a start.

"I also want all the data you've been able to find about Oscar Underwood's murder and his original investigation," Mack said. "Anything that doesn't violate the law for Iris to have. Also all traffic cam images and other data you've ever gathered about the Jackals. And the vandalism of her homeless center. Then upload a contacts list of any possible number she might need in an emergency—yours, mine, Jess's, Liam's, our buddy Noah's and his fiancée, Holly—just a wealth of people she can call when she needs help."

"You want me to preload other victim helplines, homeless shelters and useful charities?" Seth said.

"Sounds good," Mack said.

"But… I…" Iris was stammering, like her mouth couldn't figure out what words it wanted to form.

He reached out, touched her arm and squeezed it gently. "Finally," he said, "I want you to set up a debit card and add it to the phone. Link it to a brand-new bank account in Iris's name. I've got $3,250 in my emergency savings account. Transfer that into Iris's account. And make sure you have it ready by the time we reach my vehicle. Got it?"

Seth's eyes widened. "Yeah, I got it but—"

"Can you do it?" Mack pressed.

"Of course!" Seth said. "But what about—"

"Great," Mack said. "Do it."

"But I thought the plan was to bring Iris in!"

"Not anymore," Mack said. "Not unless that's what she decides she wants."

He ended the call and turned back to Iris.

"It's just a start," he said, "and it's not enough. But it's the best I can do for now. I also have a duffel bag of things in my vehicle. I packed it for you yesterday. Some clothes your size I thought you'd like, some food, toiletries, prepaid credit cards and gift cards to your favorite restaurants and stores. Also a few hundred in cash."

A small town loomed ahead. They drove past a smattering of buildings, most closed. There was a small gas station, a diner with a flickering orange sign and what looked like a cross between a hardware and grocery store. Then the buildings disappeared in the distance behind them.

Mack took a deep breath and ran his hand over the

back of his neck. "The problem I can't figure out how to solve quite yet is how to get you wheels," he said. "Neither of us should keep driving around in this thing. But I don't like the idea of giving you my undercover SUV either. But if you've got an idea, I'm all ears."

"Stop!" She grabbed his hand. He started to pull it away, but she squeezed it long and hard before letting him go. "What do you think you're doing?"

"What I should've done at the diner last night," Mack said. "I'm trying to give you what you need to succeed, instead of acting like I'm the only one who knows what's good for you. All this time I've been trying to protect you without actually taking into consideration what you kept telling me you wanted to do. I don't know how long it's going to take me to figure out the mess I'm in. But I do know that I'm not the boss of you, I can't keep making decisions for you and I can't just sweep you up into my arms and carry you off to safety. You can figure out what you need for yourself. You're the strongest, kindest, most determined woman I know. You saved your own life, without my help, and then you saved mine—"

"And you saved mine," Iris cut in, "several times. We take turns."

He chuckled. "Fair enough. Just wherever you end up and whatever you decide to do, I hope you'll find a way to let me know you're okay."

"Is that what you really want me to do?" she pressed. "You want me to take my stuff and run?"

"I want you to be safe," Mack said. "I thought the safest place for you was witness protection, but that's not even an option now. I want you to get the recognition you deserved for your work and to meet with the mayor of Toronto about rebuilding the homeless center. Tell her your ideas for radically helping the country's homeless. I want you to be there when your sister has her baby. I want you to be happy and live a big, long, incredible life where nobody ever hurts you and all your dreams come true. And I want to be the guy who makes that happen for you. Even though it's clear I can't be."

The phone rang from Seth again and Iris answered it before Mack could ask her to wait.

"Uh, guys?" Seth said. "You're gonna want to pull over. We've got a major problem up ahead."

"What kind of problem?" Mack asked, but then they crested a hill and he could see the tiny spots of light clustering on the road ahead. "Please tell me it's not a roadblock."

"It's a whole lot of roadblocks," Seth said. "Word's gotten around that you were spotted at Noel's Motel and borrowed a police vehicle without asking. Your face is all over the news. They're reporting that you're armed and dangerous. They're planning an actual, on-foot manhunt. They're going to be searching every vehicle in the area for you."

Seemed like he wasn't about to make it back to his own vehicle a free man. It wouldn't make a lick of difference if he switched vehicles, hitched a ride or got Iris to drive while he hid in the trunk. They'd find him anyway. If he tried to hide out in the woods until Liam and Jess found him, he'd freeze.

After a lifetime of living in the shadows, he was out in the light and about to be found.

He turned to Iris. "I'm trapped."

ELEVEN

There was nowhere left to run. Mack closed his eyes and prayed. *Help me, Lord. I don't know what to do. I don't know where to go.* Then he felt Iris's hand brush his. He opened his eyes and turned to her. She looped her fingers through his and squeezed.

"Hey," she said. "You're Detective Mack Gray. You've gotten out of far worse, I'm sure. You're going to be okay."

Despite everything, a smile crossed his face and fresh determination filled his lungs.

"You still got us on GPS?" he asked Seth.

"Absolutely," Seth said.

"Okay, change of plans," Mack said. "We're going to ditch the vehicle in the woods outside of the last town we passed. Then we're going to hike to town and find a place to hunker down, until Liam and Jess can reach us and arrange an extraction."

"Already on it." Seth was typing.

"How long till you can get that locked burner phone working for me?" Mack asked.

"Fifteen to twenty," Seth said. "I'm hoping. Believe me, this is the first time I've ever done this before." A determined grin crossed his face. "Always fun to get the chance to try something new."

Seth's fingers were practically flying over the keyboard now. Yeah, Mack recognized that pace. The hacker only typed that fast when he was worried.

"Don't worry," Seth said. "One way or another we'll find you. We always do."

Iris pulled her hand away from Mack's, then leaned down and tightened her laces. He turned the vehicle around and started back toward town, looking for a gap in the woods where he could safely hide the squad car.

"So, where are we heading?" Mack asked.

"The Emerald Diner," Seth said. "It's not a good place. In fact, it's most certainly a sketchy place. It was actually on Iris's map, but the owner has a habit of health code violations and also racking up gambling debts and not paying them. I can see why Iris's contacts would've recommend it though, because he also has a habit of paying people cash under the table. But it's open twenty-four hours. The lights are on, it's warm and it's the kind of dive where everyone keeps their heads down and nobody minds anybody else's business. It's not a half-bad location to hide out and wait for Liam and Jess. Especially for a guy like you, Mack, who'll know how to fit in."

A guy like him. Mack frowned. Yeah, he'd spent a whole lot of time in some very horrible places. He knew how to handle low-level criminals, especially the kind who, for some quick cash, would happily forget to tell the police they'd ever seen him.

He watched as Iris tucked her hair up inside her hat and pulled it down firmly, leaving just a few wisps sneaking out around her face. She was absolutely gorgeous and even more lovely on the inside. The Emerald Diner was definitely not the place for someone like her.

It was funny. His father would've said that a woman of Iris's background and education was beneath him. In reality, Mack was the one who wasn't good enough for her. He never had been and never would be.

He told Seth they'd check in once they reached the diner. Seth assured him that the burner phone Mack had found in the squad car would be up soon, and that Liam and Jess were en route and moving quickly. Mack wasn't quite sure what people in the diner would think of a search-and-rescue helicopter landing in their town just before dawn, or what the cops manning RCMP roadblocks would think either. Would Liam and Jess find a place to land nearby? Or just drop a ladder down outside the diner and dramatically airlift them both to safety?

Either way, once his team arrived their adventure would be over. He'd go into hiding and find somewhere to lie low while they figured out who'd framed him for Oscar's murder. Iris would have to figure out where she was going and what her next steps were. And he'd have to say goodbye.

He drove the vehicle as deep into the woods as he could without damaging it, then he and Iris worked together to cover it with branches and snow. Thankfully a white car in snow would take a while to find and once they were safe and far away from the area, he'd get Seth to call in the tip, just in case it hadn't been found.

They jogged through the woods back to the town. Bracing wind stung their skin. The air was so cold it hurt to breathe. Even in gloves, his fingers grew so numb that he couldn't even hold her hand. And the temperature kept dropping. He prayed with every step, searching the skies above for rescue and the road on the other side of the trees for danger.

Finally the first few buildings of the derelict town came into view. They stumbled from the trees and ran through back alleys until they reached the Emerald Diner.

He pushed through a back maintenance door with Iris one step behind him, and came out into a dingy hallway that led to a kitchen. The smell of freshly cooked food, heavy-duty industrial cleanser and garbage filled his nostrils at once. Still, he stopped, turned and opened his arms for Iris, and she fell into them. He hugged her hard and she hugged him back, as the damp heat slowly thawed their limbs.

Finally, he forced himself to step back and let her go. He glanced at the phone.

"No Seth yet," he said.

"What do we do now?" she asked.

"We go into the dining room, order something and act like we belong there," he said. "Then we wait. The more we look like we have nothing to hide, the better."

She unzipped her coat and pulled her gloves and hat

off. He reached for her hand and felt her fingers slip against his palm.

"Come on," he said. "Let's go find something to eat."

They walked through the back hallway into the restaurant. He stood beside Iris and scoped out the room.

About twenty people sat on cracked plastic seats, hunched over stained white mugs. There were only two exits, the front door and the back they'd come through. More people than he'd have expected at four thirty in the morning, but places open at this hour were few and far between on the highway. He didn't see anybody he recognized but many who set his cop instincts firing. This crowd wasn't the kind to mind somebody else's business and call the cops on a stranger, at least until there was a reward on his head.

A large man with a bored scowl lurked behind the counter. Mack draped his arm protectively around Iris, as he found his own shoulders hunching, lips curling and chin jutting. Stepping into the type of role he'd played almost every day for a decade, until he'd been given the opportunity to be the kind of man who'd help a social worker and volunteer at a homeless shelter.

"Eggs, sandwiches and fries only before seven," the man at the counter barked. "Nothing from the lunch or dinner menu. Anything from the deep fryer is gonna be twenty minutes. Sit anywhere."

Mack tilted his head toward him in a kind of half nod he'd learned over the years. It covered a lot of conversation. He and Iris headed for a table beside the wall. An exhausted-looking woman dropped two menus on the table and poured them cups of coffee before disappearing again.

Then it was just him and Iris.

He set the phone from the cop car face up on the table and waited for Seth's call. She fished the lone container of milk from a bowl of packaged creamers and handed it to him. Then she added two sugars and one cream to her coffee, looked for a spoon, and when she didn't see one, just swirled the cup around. She took a sip. Then her eyes met his, he felt a grin cross his face, and he remembered how many of his mornings had started out like this in those weeks he'd been targeting her for information, becoming her friend and falling in love with her all at once.

How could he let her go without a fight? How could he just accept that they were going different directions without telling her that he wanted to have a real relationship with her, even if he had no idea how or where that could possibly happen?

I can't lose her again, Lord. And I can't hide behind secret identities anymore either. It's time to be real. I have to be brave enough to live a life where I'm not disappearing into cover stories and pretending to be someone I'm not. I need to stop pushing people away and be the real authentic me, with Iris by my side.

He reached across the table toward her. "Iris—"

The power cut out, plunging the diner into darkness. Voices shouted. Thick, arid smoke filled the air.

"Everybody down!" One voice rose above them all. "This is a robbery!"

There, filling the doorway, his snarling mask illuminated in the eerie glow of a flashlight beam, was the green-masked Jackal.

A second smoke bomb exploded and heavy smoke filled Iris's lungs. Voices shouted and cursed in the darkness, mingling with the sound of some kind of siren. How had the Jackal found her? Was he still after her even though Oscar Underwood was dead? But why else had he stepped out of the shadows for a masked robbery?

For a moment she sat frozen with panic, feeling too lost in the chaos to move or even scream. Then a strong arm wrapped protectively around her shoulders and pulled her down underneath the table.

"Listen to me, Iris," Mack said. "It's going to be okay. I'll get us out of here."

"This doesn't make any sense!" Her words flew out in a rush. "Why is a Jackal here? How did he find me? Why is he robbing the diner?"

"I don't know," Mack said. "We'll find out. We'll figure all of this out. But right now what matters most is getting out of here in one piece."

Faint gray starlight seeped weakly through the huge diner windows. Already her eyes were beginning to adjust to the darkness.

The Jackal was waving a semiautomatic weapon and a flashlight while he yelled at people to toss their wallets and cell phones toward the door. He warned them all not to try anything funny.

So far not a single shot had been fired. But the air seethed and surged with tension, like a powder keg about to erupt. She'd seen this kind of uneasy calm before, when one person would threaten violence in a bar, party or wherever else she'd rushed to help get someone out after they'd called her for help.

It wouldn't last long. Someone would rush the door. Either the Jackal or someone else would fire. One way or another, a brawl would break out, shots would be fired, and the dark and smoke would only add to the chaos. People would get hurt and maybe even die.

Mack reached up, grabbed his coffee and downed it in one gulp. Then he dropped back down to her side. "Okay, time to go. Follow me. We'll take the back door."

He placed his hand on her shoulder, sheltering her with his body. They made their way along the very edge of the room, sticking close to the wall, staying low and using tables as cover. Between the darkness, thick smoke and Mack's protective cover, she could barely see anything that was happening. Just flashes of light and the snarl of the green-masked Jackal appearing and disappearing in the darkness as he made his threats.

Mack urged her on, leading her from the shelter of one overturned table to the next, stopping and starting, darting through gaps in the chaos. The entrance to the back hallway loomed ahead, a gaping hole offering escape and freedom.

Mack stopped and dropped low behind the waitress station.

"We're almost there," he said. "We'll make it out of this and keep running. Then we'll regroup and find a way to contact my team. It's all going to be okay."

She braced herself to sprint.

Then she felt a sting in the back of her leg, like a bee or a wasp, only sharper, more painful than any sting she'd ever felt before. She cried out and fell forward onto her hands and knees. She looked back but there was no one there. Then she ran her hand over her calf and felt the smooth cylinder and feathered tip of a Jackal's tranquilizer dart. She grabbed Mack's arm.

"I've been shot in the leg!" She gasped a sob. "With a tranquilizer dart."

"Where did it come from?" Mack whispered urgently.

"I don't know! Behind us somewhere!"

A prayer for God's help ripped from his lips. His eyes scanned the room and her gaze followed. She didn't see any other Jackals, except the green-masked one still barking orders. But there had to be more than one in this place and she was still their target.

Unconsciousness lapped at the edges of her mind, like gentle waves threatening to pull her under. Her heart pounded frantically. Panic filled her lungs. She pushed herself to her feet quickly, only to stumble back.

"Iris!" Mack's arm wrapped around her protectively. "Focus. You're going to stay awake, and I'll get you out of here. I promise."

The sound of motors rose high above the chaos around her. It was a helicopter. Rescue was coming.

"Thank You, God," Mack prayed. His arm tightened around her "That'll be our ride. We've just got to get you out of here, through that door, to my team and we'll be home free."

But before he finished saying the words, a cold burst of air swept in. She looked up to see the red-masked Jackal standing in the door to the hall between her and freedom.

Her knees crumpled, and it was only Mack's strength that kept her from falling. *Help us, Lord!*

They were trapped. The green-masked Jackal was behind them, the red-masked one stood in front of them, and somewhere in the chaos lurked a third who'd hit her with the dart.

"Can you still run?" Mack's voice was urgent in her ear.

"Yeah," she said. "I think so."

For now.

"Okay," he said. "All we have to do is get you past him, out the back exit and to the helicopter. I don't want to open fire, because the last thing I want is to encourage other people to start shooting off their guns. So here's the plan, I'm going to charge the Jackal by the door and bring him to the ground. When I do that, I want you to run past me, out the back door. Don't stop. Don't look back. I'll be right behind you. Trust me. We've got this."

"And you'll be right behind me?" she asked.

"Yeah." He leaned toward her and pressed his forehead against hers. "I promise."

She inhaled deeply and breathed him in. "As long as we're together, I'm good."

"Me, too," he said.

Their lips met, and somehow for one fleeting moment, despite the fear and the chaos, she found herself believing that somehow everything was going to be all right. Mack darted out from behind the waitress station with his head low and shoulders squared. He charged, throwing himself at the red-masked Jackal. The Jackal fired, but it was too late. Mack bodychecked him hard, catching him in the center of his body and throwing him back against the ground.

"Now!" Mack shouted.

Iris gritted her teeth, pushed herself up and forced herself to run, pelting through the darkness. The tranquilizer poison turned her adrenaline to sludge in her veins. Out of the corner of her eye, she saw Mack down on the diner floor fighting against the Jackal. Then she dived down the hallway, leaving the chaos behind her and feeling her feet drag with every step.

Pale, gray early morning light filled the doorway ahead of her. A large black helicopter was landing ahead of her in the snow. Mack's team was here. She was going to make it. They were both going to make it.

A second dart pierced the skin at the back of her neck. She screamed and stumbled forward, falling to her hands and knees. Two. She'd been struck with two tranquilizer darts. *Help. Me. Lord!* Her body hit the hall floor. Fresh poison swept over her. She pressed herself up to her feet. Mack! She had to tell Mack! She spun back and dizziness engulfed her. Her legs collapsed beneath her. She fell back to the floor.

Then she felt a hand grab her arm.

"Come on." The voice was female, reassuring and familiar. "We've got to go."

Was that Mack's colleague Jess?

Then she felt another hand. This one was bigger and stronger, sliding up her arms and pulling her to her feet. Then came another voice, deep and familiar. "I've got her."

Was that Liam?

"Come on, Missy," he said. "Just a few more steps."

They were pulling her, propelling her down the hallway and out into the early light. She turned and looked at her rescuers. But her eyelids felt so heavy that even away from the smoke and darkness she could barely see the faces that swam before her eyes.

"We've got her," said the woman holding her arm.

No, it wasn't Jess. This woman was much younger and taller with dyed red hair, with huge eyes in her thin face.

Iris blinked. "I know you…"

It was one of the street youth who'd warned Iris about the Jackals. The nickname she'd usually gone by was Sadie, but Iris had never found out her real name. Iris just knew that she'd once managed to escape and get to Iris for help after being sedated by the Jackals, and had then gone missing and had never been found.

"Come on," said the man holding Iris, "we've got to get her in the copter."

Iris glanced to her left. The man had a dark, buzzed haircut and a square build. She recognized him, too. He'd gone by Bowser or Big Guy and was yet another of the people whom the Jackals had kidnapped. Two of the very same kids who'd gone missing and that she'd worried about were here, and they were rescuing her?

Iris's head swam. This couldn't be real. She had to be hallucinating.

"I've been looking for you…" she murmured through heavy lips.

The rumbling around her grew louder. She looked up at the helicopter, looming ahead of her like a huge prehistoric insect. A couple of other figures, barely more than blurs to her now, were sprinting toward the helicopter from around the front of the building. They leaped into the helicopter ahead of her.

"Mack… I can't go without Mack…"

But the helicopter was growing closer. Then another pair of hands pulled her inside while another pushed her from behind.

"Iris! Hang on, I'm coming!"

Mack's voice drifted toward her from somewhere in the distance, shouting to her, calling to her, telling her he was coming, asking her to wait. But the poison's grip on her mind was too thick. The hands shoving her onto the seat were too strong.

"Iris!" Mack shouted.

"Wait…" she tried to shout. "I need Mack…"

She felt the helicopter rise, taking her away and leaving Mack behind.

The seat jolted beneath her, tossing her sideways. Her head smacked against something hard. Unconsciousness swept over her again and this time it pulled her under.

TWELVE

Iris was gone. She'd been kidnapped.

Mack stood in the snow, staring up into the sky, feeling as if a piece of his heart had been ripped from his chest.

When he'd finally subdued the red-masked Jackal, depriving him of his weapon and handcuffing him to a railing, Mack had barely paused before pelting down the hallway after Iris. But it was too late. The helicopter door had already been closing in front of him.

Now, he stood outside and alone on the snowy ground and watched, grief filling his body, as the helicopter rose above him, taking Iris farther and farther into the sky.

The phone rang. Relief hit Mack so hard he nearly fell to his knees.

He answered. "Seth!"

The hacker breathed a prayer of thanksgiving. "I heard about the robbery. Tell me you've made it out of the diner and that you're both still alive."

"Yes, but Iris has been abducted!" Mack practically shouted into the phone.

"How?" Panic filled the hacker's voice.

"A helicopter!" Mack said. One that even now was disappearing above the tree line into the early morning sky. "The wrong helicopter!"

He gasped as the full magnitude of what he was about to tell Seth hit him. Shock filled his core.

Come on, man, focus! He was still a cop at heart, who'd just escaped a mass robbery and a potential hostage situation. He had a job to do. Crisis triage was all that mattered now.

He glanced back at the diner. The door he'd burst through had swung closed behind him. Judging by the chaos of disembodied voices, several of the people the green-masked Jackal had been holding hostage had managed to slip out the front of the building, but for now he was alone behind the diner. He prayed that everyone still inside was safe, then he stepped behind a dumpster to stay hidden from anyone who made it out the back.

"Contact the RCMP and report Iris James's disappearance as an active abduction and kidnapping situation," he said. "The helicopter is black, luxury model, no logo or distinctive markings. My guess is it's someone's personal craft."

Mack could hear Seth typing even as he rambled off the technical specifications and potential models as best he could.

"On it," Seth said. "Report sent."

"Tell me there are cops en route to the Emerald

Diner," Mack said. "We have an armed robbery situation with at least two still active hostiles. Plus a third I disarmed and managed to handcuff to a railing. Don't have a description other than five foot eleven, male, about a hundred and thirty pounds. It was too dark for a positive identification."

Seth took in a long breath. The clatter of the keys kept flying down the phone. "Done," Seth said. "Several people already called the diner robbery in. I just placed an additional call and gave them additional information and to be on the look for a handcuffed Jackal. Anonymous of course."

"Thank you," Mack said. *And thank You, God.*

The tiny speck of the helicopter that had abducted Iris had disappeared over the horizon, taking the last flicker of hope in Mack's chest with it.

"What happened?" Seth said.

"We got to the diner," Mack said. "Someone cut the power, the place went dark and smoke bombs went off. The green-masked Jackal blocked the front entrance with a semiautomatic and a flashlight, claiming it was an armed robbery. Iris got hit with a tranquilizer dart. I subdued the red-masked Jackal and handcuffed him. Someone dragged Iris into a helicopter."

And now she was gone, and he had no way to follow.

"I'm so sorry." Pain pushed through Seth's voice. "I wish I'd managed to connect to your phone faster. I feel like I let you down."

"Don't blame yourself," Mack said. "I don't. Where are Liam and Jess?"

"I don't know," Seth said. "That's the other thing

I've been dealing with. Liam and Jess hit a major snag. There was some unusual aerial activity in the area so they had to drop in the woods. Then they suddenly went dark. I've been trying to find them, but they're completely gone."

Mack groaned. "I'll ask you again—are you absolutely sure Oscar Underwood is dead?"

"Liam got a friend on the inside to make a positive corpse identification," Seth said. "Irrefutable. Whoever abducted Iris and whoever the Jackals are working for now, it's not him."

The blare of sirens filled the air. Mack counted the noise of at least half a dozen cars and two ambulances blending together. There was the screech of tires, the babble of voices and the barking of orders. Somewhere in front of the diner, the authorities had arrived and were taking charge of the situation.

"Small comfort, I know," Seth said. "But I've managed to hack into the diner's security camera feed. Between the smoke bombs and the darkness, it's an absolute nightmare. But I should have footage of Iris's abduction soon."

"The cavalry has arrived," Mack said. He squared his shoulders and stepped out into the snow. "I'm going to go turn myself in."

"Uh, no!" Seth said. "That would be a very bad idea. Liam and Jess are missing in action. And have you forgotten that you've been wrongfully accused of murder? The police are going to arrest you, slap you in handcuffs and toss you in jail."

"I know," Mack said. There was a sour taste in the

back of his throat as he thought about every single thing giving himself up to police could mean. "But they'll hopefully also hear what I have to say about Iris and launch a major search for her. So, I have to do it. For Iris. If there's even a possibility that the RCMP can find her, I have to help."

"How much help are you going to be to her if you walk into a trap?" Seth asked.

"You think I don't know how much danger I'm in?" Mack said. "Nothing makes sense right now. I've got unanswered questions piling up around me and everything I thought I knew about what's going on is unraveling. But I can't be arrogant enough to think I'm the only cop out there who can help her. The one thing I know for absolute certain is that Iris is the best thing to ever happen to my life and that I will do whatever it takes to keep her safe."

He strode out into the wide-open space behind the diner and looked up at the sky. Red and blue lights flickered in the sky above him.

He'd spent his entire life hiding behind a mask. He'd been comfortable there and he'd felt safe there. But Iris had pulled all that away, just as easily as she'd removed the itchy prosthetics from his face just a few hours ago, leaving his heart open wide. And as much as he didn't want to be the public spectacle of a millionaire's son and a cop arrested for murder, as much as he dreaded being locked away with the very criminals he'd spent his life taking down, and as much as he didn't much look forward to all the different ways it would mean he'd have to fight for his life from here on in, there was one possibility he hated even more.

The possibility of life without Iris.

"Hands up! Down on the ground!" A male voice rang with authority behind him. It was strong and deep, and left no doubt that it expected to be obeyed. "Drop your weapons!"

Well, this was it then. It was too late now for any more debate. Mack's hands rose. He felt the phone fall from his fingers into the snow and tossed his gun after it. He was finally done hiding.

"Turn!" the male voice barked. "Nice and slow. Keep your hands where I can see them. Detective Mack Gray, you're under arrest for kidnapping, destruction of property and conspiracy to commit murder."

Interesting grab bag of charges. "It's my duty to inform you that you have the right to retain and instruct counsel without delay."

Mack turned toward the wall of officers approaching behind him, raising his hands high and surrendering his life into God's hands. Then his eyes rose to the face of the tall, broad-shouldered, uniformed cop, whose fierce, unsmiling gaze was fixed squarely on Mack as he pointed the weapon at him. It was only the threat of the very many other armed men and women around them that kept Mack from bursting out into laughter.

Instead he dropped to his knees, placed his hands on his head and thanked God under his breath as Detective Liam Bearsmith, one of the best cops he'd ever had the privilege of working with, strode toward him, reciting Mack's rights.

"Hey," Mack murmured under his breath as Liam stepped between him and the onlookers.

"Good to see you," Liam said softly. "Where's Iris?"

"Kidnapped. Helicopter."

Liam breathed a prayer under his breath.

"Where's Jess?" Mack asked.

"Managing transportation." Liam grabbed Mack's hands and clasped the handcuffs on.

"Nice touch," Mack said. "But are these really necessary?"

"Yup," Liam said. "A lot of people want you behind bars. Others want you dead and there are camera phones everywhere. We're not out of the woods yet."

He scooped up Mack's cell phone and weapon. Then he grabbed Mack by the elbow and hauled him to his feet. Liam walked him around the side of the diner and Mack suddenly realized just how large a crowd had gathered.

There were dozens of cops and patrons, engaged in more than one heated discussion. He saw a few stretchers, but no major injuries or body bags. He counted at least a dozen phones shooting footage. He wondered how long it would take video of his arrest to appear on the news and what his parents would think.

"Keep your eyes on the ground." Liam bent Mack's head down, shielded his face with his elbow and marched him through the crowd. "Look defeated."

"Any fatalities?" Mack asked quietly.

"Nope," Liam said. "Few minor injuries but nothing major."

"I caught one Jackal and handcuffed him to a railing so he wouldn't escape while I was helping Iris," Mack said.

"Hadn't heard about that," Liam said. "Jess might. Or he might've gotten free before police showed up. There's talk of robbery, but officially I think it's going to go down as some kind of a brawl caused by the power outage."

"But people saw a masked Jackal demanding wallets."

"An owner with a history of breaking the law and a bunch of people who've got warrants out for their own arrests isn't a combo likely to result in a whole lot of positive identifications," Liam said. "These are the kind of people who avoid helping police because they don't want their own stuff accidentally slipping out. Do you think the Jackals wanted to cause a diversion to kidnap Iris?"

"I do now," Mack said. "There were two Jackals I saw, plus someone got Iris with a tranquilizer dart. Did they at least get the Jackal in the green mask who was robbing the place?"

"That I can't tell you," Liam said. "Again, maybe Jess knows."

They reached one cop car among many, Liam opened the back door, shoved him in, did up his seat belt and slammed the door behind him. Mack looked up. Jess was in the driver's seat. Like Liam, she was also in full uniform. Her eyes met his and the corner of her lips twitched in the subtlest of smiles.

"They got Iris," Liam told her, climbing into the passenger seat before Mack could even speak. Liam shut the door behind him and snapped on his seat belt.

Mack noticed the eyes and cell phones followed every move.

"I'm sorry," Jess said. Her eyes cut to the rearview mirror as she put the car in Drive. "Don't worry, Mack. We'll figure out where she is and get her back. For now, just try to look like a man who's just been arrested for his crimes until we get out of here. I guarantee people will be recording us driving off and the car might still be searched."

He nodded and slumped back in his seat, his head bowed. The vehicle pulled away through the chaos of people, vehicles and flashing lights.

"Seth said you went dark," Mack said.

"Yeah," Liam said. "We didn't want to risk being caught. In fact, he doesn't yet know we have you."

It wouldn't be the first time witness protection police officers hadn't kept their civilian computer tech in the loop, but considering how much he complained, they included him whenever they could.

"We were picked up at a police checkpoint," Liam went on, "and after that we weren't alone long enough to risk it. Right now there's a very senior RCMP officer wandering around the diner crime scene, wondering why the two officers he kindly drove to the diner didn't tell him before taking his car."

Something in Liam's relaxed tone made Mack think

that while he regretted the fact he'd have to apologize to a colleague, he wasn't worried they'd get in any trouble for it.

"Risky move," Mack said. "Want to tell me how you two managed to pull this off?"

"I have friends in this area," Liam said. "Ones that were incredibly thankful for the tips a few hours back that led to the major raid at Crow's Farm. They owed me one for your intel on that, not that I ever expected I'd have to call it in so quickly."

"They agreed to let you smuggle me out of here?" Mack asked. Yes, Liam had a stellar reputation and cops across the country owed a lot to his help. But letting someone just dodge arrest was a bridge too far.

"Of course not." Liam chuckled. "They agreed to let me be the one to arrest you and bring you in."

Yeah, that made more sense.

"You going to get me out of these handcuffs?" Mack asked. "And call Seth?"

"Not yet," Liam said. "Not until we're out of here."

Liam's somber eyes met Mack's in the rearview mirror. "And don't worry, besides getting you out of here, our own priority is finding Iris and getting her back safe. We will find her. I give you my word."

A checkpoint loomed ahead. Jess slowed the vehicle and flashed her badge and the warrant for Mack's arrest. A police officer shone a flashlight through the back window at the vehicle at him. Mack scowled, hung his head and did his best impression of a corrupt and entitled cop whose crimes had finally caught up with him. Then he held his breath and waited as Liam and the cop outside chatted for a moment. They were finally waved through.

The checkpoint disappeared in the distance. Trees and sky surrounded them on all sides.

Liam leaned forward and pressed a button on the screen. Seth's face appeared, looking panicked. The hacker's mouth opened like he was about to say something, but then his eyes took in the scene. Then he burst out laughing.

The sound was so spontaneous and freeing that an odd feeling of relief moved through Mack's limbs, mingling with the anguish in his core. He wasn't alone anymore. His team was here. They'd find Iris. They had to.

"I feel like I just looked away from the movie at the wrong moment and missed a whole chunk of the plot," Seth said.

"Long story short," Liam said, "we got caught by a roadblock, went dark, pulled in a favor with the team who raided Crow's, and then we arrested Mack."

"Hang on," Mack said. "I'm not actually arrested, am I?"

"Did he read you your rights?" Jess asked, with a slight smile. "Because there's a very real warrant out for your arrest and he is a cop."

"I haven't filed the paperwork yet," Liam said. He opened the partition window to the back seat and tossed a pair of handcuff keys into Mack's fingers.

"You're not going to uncuff me?" Mack asked.

"Not unless you actually need me to," Liam said, with a grin.

Mack rolled his eyes and started working on the

cuffs, thankful for the distraction of having something to do with his hands. "How's the security footage coming along?"

"I have blurry images of a man and a woman helping Iris up and escorting her to the helicopter," Seth said. "They don't match anyone in our database."

It was a start. But not as much of one as he'd have hoped for.

"Please tell me that police have arrested the green- and red-masked Jackals," he said.

"It's still a crime scene in progress," Seth said. "More arrests will be coming. But for right now, there's no record of anyone being arrested matching their description, unless you guys know something I don't."

Seth glanced to Jess and Liam. Both shook their heads. Mack yanked his hands free from the handcuffs.

"I handcuffed the red-masked Jackal to a railing inside the diner," he said. "Someone will have to have a cell phone picture of him at least."

"On it." Seth was typing. "Also, no hit on the helicopter yet. Yes, I know that people are supposed to file flight plans, but..."

"But someone pulled some strings somewhere," Mack supplied, "and so far you can't figure out where all those tugs are coming from."

Mack closed his eyes and prayed. *Lord, this whole thing just feels like a setup. But whatever it is, I just can't see it.*

Sometimes it helped to go right back to the start.

"My father always taught me that everything comes down to connections and networks," Mack said. The irony finally hit him that for all the "connections" he'd made in his life, only a few, like his team, had been real. And only one, Iris, had gotten through to his core. "For him, it was business networks. For us, it's criminal networks and the law enforcement community. When I met Iris, it was because the RCMP was investigating whether Oscar Underwood's criminal activity was being enabled by corruption within the Toronto police or just negligence. The facts pointed to a potential conspiracy, only I found no proof of criminality or corruption. Even the cops wanting to arrest me now are just doing their jobs."

Liam nodded.

"There's a network of street youth and homeless people, too," Mack went on. "A lot of the people who live on the streets know each other or the places to go. Iris kept one step ahead of the Jackals using a map of safe places that people at her homeless center had helped her create. But somehow it still led us to a criminal enterprise. And no matter where she ran, the Jackals kept finding her. Which implies she's being pursued by someone who knows about the map, or at least the locations on it. But none of that seems to connect to anything."

More nods.

"Finally," he said, "Iris was kidnapped by an expensive and unmarked helicopter. That means she was abducted by either someone with money or someone who has access to very expensive toys. Definitely not law enforcement, too nice to belong to Crow or most criminals I know, and I can't believe it belongs to a street kid. How are the police, the wealthy and the homeless connected? And what does that have to do with someone sedating and kidnapping Iris?"

"Is this the guy you were fighting with?" Seth asked.

Mack looked up at the blurry picture of a man in dark fatigues and a red ski mask pulled up off his thin face. "Yeah, that's him. Very vaguely familiar, but I can't really see his face. Got a match?"

"Not yet." Seth kept typing.

"Can I see the picture of the two people who abducted Iris?" Mack asked.

"Sure, but I haven't managed to clean it up yet," Seth said.

The picture appeared on the screen. He didn't recognize the figures, but Iris didn't seem to be fighting them either.

"There's something else I'm missing," Mack said. "These people actually managed to take her. Iris is the most tenacious person I've ever met. Even sedated, I can't imagine her ever just meekly leaving with a stranger."

"She wouldn't have left without you," Liam said softly, and yet the words seemed to strike Mack somewhere deep inside his core. "You're talking about a woman who dragged you into a camper when you were sedated and refused to leave Crow's Farm when you were taken inside. If Jess and I had shown up and tried to take her away without you, she'd have fought tooth and nail to not leave without you. So, whoever took her was able to catch her off guard long enough to kidnap her."

"So, she knew them?"

He closed his eyes. *Help me, Lord. None of the pieces fit.* Iris lived her life surrounded by a community of people who were poor and in need. They loved her, and she loved them. None were the kind who flew around in expensive helicopters. Words he and Iris had said to each other floated at the corners of his minds.

There's more than one way to be rich. And more than one way to be poor.

"Seth." Mack opened his eyes. "What about the pictures of street kids from the homeless center? The ones that weren't found in the raids on Underwood's properties?"

"I haven't managed to get a hit on those yet either," Seth said. "Why?"

"Okay, I might have a theory," Mack said. "There were some kids that saw the Jackals and were terrified of them. In some cases, they had survived an attempted kidnaping already. They told Iris about the Jackals and then disappeared, but they weren't found when Oscar's properties were raided. Some might've gone off the grid. But what if others didn't? They were the ones who'd told her about the places on the map, so they'd know where to look for her. They might even have friends or contacts at places she'd visited, like the Emerald Diner or Crow's Farm. What if some of the same people hunting her had also helped her create her map?"

Jess glanced back at him. "So you're saying some of the people Iris helped at the homeless center are now working for the Jackals?"

"I don't know," Mack said. "Because they're terrified of the Jackals. But how many times in our work have we seen young people forced into working for criminals? If Iris were here, she'd remind us that these people were her friends and people she cared about, and that if any of them were caught up in this, they need our help. I can't imagine any of them willingly hurting Iris. They loved her. She took care of them."

It was a theory, but not a complete one.

"What are you saying?" Liam asked.

"I don't know," Mack said. He could feel the wheels in his head spinning. "Seth, try matching the red-masked Jackal against the photos Iris had up in her camper?"

Almost immediately he heard a ping.

Seth gasped. "Well, what do you know?" he said. "We got an overlap. The red-masked Jackal was in one of Iris's pictures from the homeless center."

Mack leaned back against his seat. Okay, he didn't know what it meant yet, but he had something. "How about the two people who ushered Iris into the helicopter?"

"Already on it," Seth said. Moments later his machine pinged again. "Yup, they're from the homeless center pictures, too. They're all street youth who weren't found in the Underwood raids."

Mack blew out a hard breath. Okay, so that could explain how the Jackals kept finding Iris and how they'd gotten her into the helicopter. But not why. Why would they turn against Iris and help criminals kidnap her?

Who possibly had that power over them? How did this tie into Oscar's murder?

"How do we find out who they are?" Mack asked.

"First off, a hasty picture you took of a printed photo isn't the easiest thing for facial recognition software to do much with," Seth said. "Even for me. Same for these new blurry pictures from the Emerald Diner. But at least we have more data to go on than we did an hour ago. I ran the pictures against missing persons and the crime database. Whoever those people are, they've never been arrested or charged with anything, and they've never been reported missing. Which in itself is suspicious, considering Iris met them when they were living on the streets and in shelters. So we have young people who ended up homeless and in need without ever having a brush with the law or being reported missing by a loved one. It makes no sense."

Unless they were connected to the kind of person who made arrests go away and cared more about avoiding scandal than reporting a missing child.

Someone like Mack's father and his wealthy contacts. Maybe the connection between the young people was that they all came from families with money.

"Try high school yearbooks," Mack said. "Private ones. The more exclusive and expensive the better."

His father had taught him that everything came down to networks. He'd just been searching the wrong ones. Jess pulled off the main road and onto a smaller path, then he saw a yellow rescue helicopter on a concrete square ahead of them.

"Got it!" Seth slapped the desk in front of him with

both hands so hard that he nearly pushed himself up out of his seat. "Joseph Peterson, aged twenty-five, is the red-masked Jackal. Sara Ford, aged eighteen, and Elliot Jones, aged twenty-eight, are the ones who helped Iris into the helicopter."

"What existing points of contact do they have outside the homeless center?" Liam asked. "Same school? Same employer? Same treatment facility for drugs or alcohol? Anything to give us a clue as to who they're working with, why they'd still want to kidnap Iris after Oscar Underwood was killed and where they'd be keeping her now?"

"Nothing I can see," Seth said.

But Mack knew someone who might.

"How wealthy are their families?" Mack asked.

"Hang on," Seth said. "Just tracking their parents now…and they're all pretty rich. Definitely in the top one percent. Multiple houses, country clubs, big businesses…"

Thank You, God. They might finally have a lead.

"So, they're all from wealthy families," Mack said. "And when it comes to people with money, I know someone with an encyclopedic knowledge of how they are connected. I need to make a call."

Liam leaned back and dropped his phone into his hand.

Mack took the phone and dialed the one number he'd always know from memory. Determination swept through him as he prayed.

The phone clicked.

"Mackenzie!"

"Hi, Mom."

"Are you okay?" His mother's voice was breathless and filled to the brim with emotion. "Where are you? Your face is all over the news!"

"He's been arrested, hasn't he?" His father's voice filtered in from somewhere behind his mother. "I told you we'd be his one call. What does he need? A lawyer? Bail? Whatever it is, you tell him he's not going to get it."

Mack gritted his teeth and swallowed back his own pride.

Lord, I'm never going to know what led my father to become the man he is today. Or what wounds and challenges he's faced. Help me to remember that in his own way, he is very poor, and in some ways I am rich.

"Mom, listen to me," Mack said. "I'm fine. The cops around me are really good people, and it's all going to be sorted out soon. I need you to put me on speaker phone. Can you do that for me?"

"Okay, but your dad doesn't want to speak to you..." she began.

"I know." Mack just hoped he'd stick close enough to the phone to listen.

The phone clicked again.

"I know... I know... Patrick," his mother was saying. "But he insisted."

"I met someone," Mack jumped in, "she's amazing, Mom, and I really hope I can introduce you to her. You'll love her. Dad, I hope you'll see all the amazing ways she's better than me. She's in really bad trouble. I can't explain. But her life's in danger, and I need Dad's help to save her.

"You know I've never asked you for anything," Mack said. "I've been too proud and stubborn. But right now I need information to save her life. That's all I need, just information about people Dad knows, and it's urgent. I need to know what the grown children of three wealthy families have in common."

His father was muttering under his breath. Mack could picture him standing there, arms crossed, shaking his head.

"Dad, you have encyclopedic memory when it comes to people in your sphere and how they're connected," Mack plowed on. "I've always admired your ability to remember facts about people. It's something we share. Right now, I've got to find a connection between Joseph Peterson, Sara Ford and Elliot Jones. I'm sure you know everything there is to know about their families, their parents and their businesses. Come on, Dad. There's something connecting them. I don't know what. But the life of the woman I care about most in the world depends on my figuring it out and fast. Do you know what it is?"

He closed his eyes and prayed hard. The work he'd done in the past filled his mind along with all the vital pieces of information he'd pried out of difficult places.

Please, Lord, help me find Iris.

"Dad, I've never asked you for anything. But, please, I don't want to live without her."

Then he heard his father clear his throat.

* * *

Mack! Help me, Lord, I need to save him!

The singular thought shot through Iris's sedated mind, jolting her back to consciousness.

She was lying down. The world seemed to sway gently, and she was so groggy that for a moment she couldn't even open her eyes. Warmth filled her limbs, but she wasn't wearing her coat, hat, mitts or boots. Then she opened her eyes and blinked slowly as the room around her came into focus.

She was lying on a couch in an office. The space wasn't large, yet it was lavish and comfortable with warm, cream-colored walls. The faint pink of sunrise showed through oval windows on one side. Rows of smiling student pictures were mounted on the wall behind an antique desk. It was oddly familiar, and yet she knew she was somewhere she'd never been before.

Lord, where am I? And how do I get out of here? Her mouth and throat were so dry she felt like she'd been inhaling sawdust. She tried to sit up, but her head felt heavy and a headache overwhelmed her. Tears filled her eyes.

Disjointed memories filtered through her mind like a slow-motion nightmare she couldn't escape. Jackals had invaded the diner... She'd been hit with two tranquilizer darts... Some of the street youth she'd been worried about had appeared and helped her escape...

No, that couldn't be right. Was it? What would they have been doing there?

And she'd left Mack behind.

Fresh tears rushed to the corners of her eyes. His face filled her mind. She saw the determined wrinkle he got between his eyes when he was focused on something and the soft lines that twitched at the corner of his mouth when he was fighting the urge to laugh. She remembered the way his shoulders tensed whenever he sensed danger, how his hands rose instinctively when he was prepared to fight, and the million little ways he made her feel safe and protected, from brushing a hand on her back to pulling her close to his side.

When Mack hugged her, it was like he was gathering up all their broken parts and squeezing them back together. She couldn't remember a time when she hadn't thought she was falling in love with him, even if she hadn't been ready to admit it to herself.

She sat up so quickly she nearly fell back down. Instead, Iris gritted her teeth, dragged her legs over the edge of the couch and pressed her hands into her knees, forcing herself to stay seated upright.

There was a door at the end of the couch, with pale light shining through a glass window at the top. Fear stabbed her heart. Through the window, she caught a glimpse of the strong, unrelenting bulk of the green-masked Jackal guarding the door.

Any tiny sliver of hope that she wasn't actually someone's prisoner seeped from her.

Her jacket was slung over a chair by the door and her boots under it. She shoved her feet into the boots and pushed her arms through the sleeves of her coat. Then she saw the clock, large and ornate, hanging on the wall behind her. She blinked. It was seven thirty.

It had been over two-and-a-half hours since she'd been sedated. And Mack hadn't found her yet. Which meant either she'd been very well hidden or something really bad had happened to Mack.

Looked like it was up to her to find something she could use as a weapon, get the Jackal to open the door, take him out and escape.

Then she'd find Mack.

Iris pushed herself to her feet and stumbled toward the desk. The floor seemed to shift beneath her. There had to be something she could use to escape. She'd use the desk chair if she had to.

She heard the Jackal tell someone she was awake. Then his bulk moved away from the glass, the door swung open and a burst of cold air rushed the room as a striking woman with long and glossy gray hair strode in, clad in slacks, an expensive trench coat and heels.

"Iris! You're up! What are you doing on your feet?" The voice was caring and commanding all at once.

Iris blinked as the woman came into focus, forcing her mind to register the picture in front of her.

No... It couldn't be...

It was Lisa Kats, the mayor of Toronto.

She had to be hallucinating.

"Now, sit." The mayor gently but firmly took her arm, led her to the couch and pushed her back down. "You should be lying down. The doctor's on his way and until he gets here, I don't want to risk you getting any sicker than you already are."

The door closed behind her. Iris listened for a

latching sound and didn't hear one. Did that mean they hadn't been locked in?

"I'm not sick," Iris began. She just felt like she'd been drugged and was still not quite awake.

"Of course you're sick." Mayor Kats crossed her arms. "You got severe motion sickness in the helicopter. Don't you remember? My bodyguards had to practically carry you. I wanted to take you to the hospital, but you were determined to still meet with me and said you were feeling better and it was just airsickness. But once you got into my office, you lay down on my couch and passed out right away. So I called my personal doctor and he's on his way."

No, no, that wasn't right. She couldn't remember any of that happening.

"I need to talk to the police," Iris said.

"You already did." The mayor blinked. "Don't you remember?"

"No…" This didn't make sense. It couldn't be real.

Mayor Kats shook her head as if she was more worried than Iris was.

"When the RCMP rescued you from the hostage situation at the diner, you spoke at length to the officers on board and gave a full and complete statement." The mayor's voice grew firmer. "I've been following your situation closely, Iris, and your story really touched my heart. I understand you came from an impoverished family who have a lot of financial needs, and the center you were running for the homeless and street youth was closed. I wanted to help, so I asked to be informed immediately if you were found. When I heard police were airlifting you to safety, I insisted on coming personally to meet you at the RCMP helipad."

Then why didn't she remember talking to police or Mayor Kats coming to pick her up? Yes, she'd been hit with two tranquilizer darts, but had she really blanked out that much?

Yet, the mayor's voice was so confident, it left no doubt that she expected to be believed. Either Iris's memories were completely wrong, she was dreaming, or Mayor Kats had kidnapped her and was lying about it.

"Somebody kidnapped me," Iris said. "I'm being held prisoner. Right now, there's a masked Jackal guarding the door."

"No, no, of course not!" Mayor Kats laughed. Her smile was so wide Iris suddenly felt foolish. The mayor stood in front of her desk and her wall of smiling teenagers. She leaned back against her desk and crossed her arms. It was the posture of someone who was comfortable both with power and herself.

Iris glanced back to the door. The Jackal was gone, and Iris could see nothing but pink-streaked morning. Was she strong enough to run? If so, where would she go? And what if her memory really was wrong?

She clenched her teeth and willed her mind to clear. All those days she'd camped out in front of the mayor's office trying to get her to listen and pay attention to what really mattered… She didn't know what was more implausible, that she'd finally gotten a meeting with the mayor while being too sedated to remember it, or that the mayor had kidnapped her.

"Where's Mack Gray?" Iris asked. "I need to talk to Mack, now."

"I'm so sorry." Mayor Kats shook her head, something like compassion flooding her voice. "I was told that your kidnapper might've used some form of sedation to keep you compliant and confused."

Iris might be confused about some things, but Mack Gray was definitely not one of them.

"Where is Mack?" she repeated.

The mayor frowned. "Detective Gray has been arrested."

"For what? Paying some hit man to kill Oscar Underwood? Mack's innocent!"

"Detective Mack Gray is far from innocent." The mayor's voice grew colder and it filled the room. "He's a professional liar and con artist. He befriended you under false pretenses and fed you a steady stream of lies. He manipulated you into believing a completely ludicrous story about Oscar Underwood's henchmen sedating and kidnapping homeless people, because apparently taking a man down on employment violations wasn't a big enough case for him."

"But the Jackals were kidnapping people," Iris began.

Hadn't there been one guarding the mayor's office door just moments ago? Hadn't they kept coming after her?

The mayor continued, "Detective Gray was suspended from duty for his behavior on the Oscar Underwood case and disobeying a direct order."

"He was protecting me," Iris countered.

"Did he tell you that?" Mayor Kats asked. "I have no doubt that's what he wanted you to believe, when he tracked you down and talked you into going on the run with him. He can be very convincing."

So can you, Iris thought.

"I realize the past fourteen hours have been very difficult for you," the mayor went on. "I can't imagine how persuasive that man can be, seeing as he met you under one identity, and then when he found you and told you he was a cop, he somehow managed to manipulate you to go on the run with him in a matter of hours. But now that's over. You're safe."

Iris's head fell into her hands. No, no, none of that was true. Well, maybe parts of it were, but not in the way the mayor was spinning it and twisting it and trying to turn it into something ugly.

"You obviously have a really good heart and you care about people a lot," Mayor Kats said. "We need more people like you in our city. I get it, you want to save everyone. So do I. That's why I created my scholarship program. Detective Mack Gray took advantage of you. He didn't tell you he was from a wealthy family, did he?"

No, Mack hadn't. Maybe Mack hadn't told her the full story of his life. But she knew his heart. She knew who he was on the inside. And she trusted his feelings for her were real.

"But I saw the Jackals with my own eyes," Iris said. "There were men in masks with faces painted on them. They tried to kidnap me yesterday and they tried again at the lake in the middle of the night and sank my trailer. Then they robbed the diner this morning."

"I don't doubt you remember it that way," the mayor said. "But what I need you to do right now is forget everything that's happened since yesterday afternoon. Put it out of your mind. Pretend it didn't happen and never think of it again. Because you're right, there's been a tragedy that has impacted the most vulnerable people in the city and I need your help to set it right."

"My help?" Iris asked.

"Your help," Mayor Kats repeated. She pointed at Iris. "You're a champion for the underdog. You're the biggest heart this city has. You've been hurt by bad men, and I want to help you with that. First Oscar Underwood took advantage of some vulnerable people with some very bad employment and hiring practices that I can't endorse or get behind—"

"It was way more than that!" Iris tried to interject.

"And then the detective investigating him behaved criminally—"

"No, I'm really sure he didn't!"

Why was her head still swimming? Why did it feel like the room was rocking?

"I'll be honest," the mayor said. "I'm days away from receiving the Order of Canada for my charity work. The ceremony and media coverage will shine a huge light on the city of Toronto and our success in cleaning up the city's homelessness problem…"

But the city hadn't been cleaning up the homelessness problem. People had been disappearing.

"Getting rid of people isn't the same as helping

them!" Iris said. "Other parts of the country sent their homeless here, and Oscar abducted them and took them somewhere else. That's just getting needy people out of your sight, so you can ignore the problem. I showed up outside your office for weeks trying to get you to listen, only for your big hulking chief of security to practically shove me outside."

The corner of the mayor's mouth twitched and Iris suddenly remembered that Mack had told her that this very aggressive man the mayor had once hired as her chief of security—Travis Otis—had violated both his parole on an assault charge and a restraining order.

Something else was niggling in the back of Iris's mind. Why couldn't someone who'd built her entire reputation on helping needy youth not see it was wrong to accept glory for reducing the city's homelessness under these circumstances?

Iris looked past Mayor Kats to the near identical pictures of young people on the wall, posing with the mayor. The mayor's scholarship program was such a large part of her reputation. But somehow, seeing the rows and rows of pictures of kids standing beside the mayor with the same stiff smile on her face, they looked less like people the mayor actually had a relationship with and more like trophies.

"Let me be blunt." Mayor Kats crossed her arms. "You have a major problem. You have no job, no money, no home in the city to return to and a family who can't afford to support you. But I have a solution. I want to give you a job, with a very generous salary and housing allowance, as social awareness coordinator for the city's homeless problem. I want you out before the cameras talking all about that big heart of yours and how everyone in this city matters. I want to create new, bright, clean homeless shelters, drop-in centers and programs that you can be the face of."

For a moment something swelled in Iris's heart. She was being offered everything she ever wanted. A job she cared about, a good apartment and money to help her family.

This is everything I've prayed to You for. Why does it feel so wrong?

"I want this all nailed down so I can announce it before the ceremony," the mayor went on. "There'll be some paperwork to sign and legal matters, especially as to how you talk about the uncomfortable situation with Oscar Underwood and Mack Gray. But my lawyer can help your messaging with that. Of course, there will be some restrictions as to what kinds of things the homeless and street youth program entails and the type of people we help. We don't want the wrong kind of people causing problems for city staff. You'll have to sign a nondisclosure agreement and we'll have to carefully manage your appearances to make sure you're on point. But you'll be able to save the city. You'll be this city's champion. And everyone likes a champion."

All she had to do was agree to let the mayor control who she helped and how. Iris would get paid to make a difference the way the mayor approved and in return the mayor would have the perfect way to change the story about the entire Oscar Underwood debacle before she hit the global stage.

Help me, Lord. Help me see what I need to see.

The rising sun cast long streaks of pale light along the walls. The door couldn't be locked, could it? After all, why would the mayor's office lock from the outside? She couldn't see the green-masked Jackal anymore. But that didn't mean he hadn't been there. Or that he wasn't lurking nearby.

Iris's eyes ran to the rows of young people on the wall. And then she saw them. There, among the hundreds of pictures, were six youth she'd met through the homeless center, including the two who had pulled her into the helicopter.

"Who are they?" Iris pointed.

"The young people I've helped with my scholarship program," Mayor Kats said.

"But several of them ended up living on the streets," Iris said. "I know, because I've met them at my center. They had serious problems and needed help."

"I assure you that didn't happen." Darkness moved between the mayor's eyes. "Every single recipient of my scholarship program is now in full-time education or gainfully employed. I guarantee it. I have a one hundred percent success rate."

Something in her tone said there was no other option.

"But you can't control how someone else's life is going to turn out," Iris said. "People make mistakes. They start dating the wrong person or get addicted to painkillers or flunk out of school. So don't tell me that you don't want to help the wrong kind of people. We're all the wrong kind of people, and in need of constant help, forgiveness and grace. We all fall down a lot, and it's our job to help each other get back up."

"I'm trying to help you, Iris." The mayor scowled. "And you're being difficult. Don't make this harder than it has to be."

Iris laughed and felt fresh air fill her lungs. Oh, but she was difficult. And tenacious and scrappy and not about to let anyone tell her who she was allowed to help, how she was allowed to help them and what she was allowed to say. No, she was like a storm. And that was something she'd been proud of whenever she'd looked deep into Mack's eyes.

"I have a theory," Iris said. She stood slowly, praying her feet to hold. "And if I'm wrong, it should be fairly easy to prove. My theory is that you turned a blind eye to what Oscar Underwood was doing because it bene-fited you that he was getting the people you didn't like off the streets. I think you nudged the police to turn a blind eye to what he was doing. And when you real-ized three of your scholarship recipients were living on the streets, you were worried they'd be a blight on your success rate and reputation, so you saw Oscar's Jackals as a way to solve the problem. I think you ig-nored me for months because I was an inconvenience and now you want to use me to salvage this crisis that could ruin your career and expose you as a monster.

"But maybe I'm wrong, and if I'm wrong, it should be simple enough to prove. Take me to wherever the police are holding Mack and let me talk to him. Hold a public inquiry into what Oscar Underwood did and make it your mission to help everyone he hurt. If you really want to fix this, I'm with you. I'm on board a hundred percent. We just do it out in the open. No secrets. No nondisclosure agreements. We let it be messy and full of truth. What do you say?"

The mayor chuckled. It wasn't a nice sound.

"Yeah, that's what I thought," Iris said.

"You really think you have the upper hand here?" Mayor Kats asked. Her lips turned at the edges like she was forcing herself to taste something unpleasant. "I was offering you an opportunity to get out of this mess with your life intact. You need me more than I need you. You have nothing. You are nothing. You've lost everything. And I'm offering you the opportunity to have the kind of life you've never had while doing the work you want to do."

"And in exchange, I keep my mouth shut about Oscar Underwood," Iris said, "and let everyone believe that Mack is a criminal who manipulated me. You really don't know who I am at all if you think I can be bribed into betraying either the truth or someone I care about."

She turned and started toward the door, one step at a time.

"You think you can just walk out of here?" the mayor said sharply.

"I don't know," Iris said. "But I'm going to try."

Thankfully her legs were supporting her weight. She was feeling stronger with every step and now that she was moving, her head was clearer. She grabbed the door handle, it turned, and then fresh, cold air filled her lungs.

A gun clicked behind her. Iris turned and stared at the small handgun in Mayor Kats's hand. "Miss James, we can do this the easy way or the hard way."

"If you knew anything about me," Iris said, "you'd know I never do anything the easy way." In one swift motion, she snatched a potted plant off a table and flung it at her.

The mayor fired, her bullet missing its target and shattering the clock on the wall beside Iris's head. Pottery and earth exploded around her.

Iris yanked the door open and pelted outside. Cold air struck her face, and fear filled her core so suddenly she almost froze.

She was on a boat.

The mayor's yacht was huge. Pale blue skies spread above her and gray waters beneath her. The Toronto shoreline was a dark silhouette in the distance.

Iris turned to run, choosing a direction at random and praying she'd find a way off the boat and to shore. But before she could even move, a large man in dark fatigues and a green Jackal mask stepped out in front of her. He raised his weapon and pointed it at her.

"Down!" he bellowed, deep and loud. "Now!"

Iris's knees buckled as a whimper slipped out her lips. She was trapped. There was no way out.

"Turn around!" he ordered.

She turned back and watched as the mayor strode toward her, a small handgun in her grip. Iris felt her knees give way. She tumbled to the deck.

"How long have the Jackals been working for you?" Iris asked, looking up at the mayor. If she was going to die, here and now, trapped between the criminal pointing a gun at her back and the one he was working for in front of her, at least she was going to get answers.

"Did you go visit Oscar in jail after he was arrested and offer to help get the charges dropped if he got his guys to work for you?" Iris asked. "Or did you both have something worked out before he was arrested?"

"I might have done him a favor in return for helping me clean up the city." The mayor smirked.

Iris gasped in a deep breath of cold air and felt her head clear even further. "And in exchange for turning a blind eye to what he was doing, his Jackals kidnapped the street youth you'd given scholarships to and forced them to work for you."

"They knew the scholarship came with conditions." Anger flashed in the mayor's eyes. "I took good care of them—"

"Let me guess," Iris said. "You gave them a place to live and a job in exchange for their freedom? Then you had Oscar killed and Mack framed for it, clearing up all the loose ends but me."

The mayor smirked but didn't answer. The Jackal pressed the barrel of his gun into the back of her head.

"What do you want me to do with her?" he asked.

"Get rid of her," Mayor Kats said. "She's too much trouble alive."

Iris closed her eyes and let prayers tumble wordlessly through her mind.

The Jackal's hand landed on her shoulder.

Then he squeezed her shoulder twice.

THIRTEEN

Mack? Hope surged through Iris's heart. She glanced back and up at him, ignoring the barrel of the weapon as it brushed against her head, hoping with everything inside her to see a pair of fierce blue eyes locked on hers.

But he was staring straight ahead, and she could barely see the face beneath the mask. She had no reason to believe it was Mack. And yet...

"How do you want me to get rid of her?" he asked, his words curt, like a soldier waiting for orders.

"Kill her." Cold menace spread through the Mayor of Toronto's voice. "Take her with you, kill her somewhere remote and make sure her body's not found. I don't want any evidence she's ever been on this boat." She paced a moment, like she was brainstorming a solution. "I need the scholarship Jackals killed, as well. And make sure Mack Gray has an unfortunate run-in at the wrong end of a shank. It's the only way. We clear house completely and get rid of any potential witnesses."

The hand disappeared from Iris's shoulder.

"Got it," the man behind her said. "Kill Iris James, Mack Gray and the Jackals who received scholarships from the mayor, and make sure nothing links you to helping Oscar Underwood's Jackals drug and abduct people. You got that?"

"Yes," Mayor Kats snapped. "That's what I said!"

"I wasn't talking to you," Mack said in the dry, warm voice she'd know anywhere.

Oh, Mack, I knew it was you!

"I think he was talking to me." Seth's voice crackled from a phone speaker somewhere behind her.

Then Mack's strong arm grabbed Iris by the elbow, steering her behind him as he placed himself between her and the mayor. The mayor fired. So did Mack. Twin bullets ripped the air. But only one person fell. The mayor yelped in pain and stumbled to the ground.

Mack ripped the Jackal's mask off and she caught a glimpse of the fierce eyes and determined smile that sent hope and happiness flowing through her core.

"Come on." Mack grabbed Iris's hand and pulled her to her feet. "I know you're gonna want to help her put a compress on the wound or something. But it's only a graze. She'll be fine. And there are more people with guns on this boat to worry about."

Already she could hear the footsteps coming toward them. Her grip tightened in Mack's hand and she let him lead her down the deck. He opened a door and pulled her inside what seemed to be a cupboard, filled with life jackets and cleaning supplies. Mack slid his arms around her and pulled her close to his chest as they heard footsteps running outside.

He turned to his shoulder microphone. "How's that evacuation coming?"

"On its way," Liam's voice came back. "Just hold on."

Mack let out a sigh of relief and hugged Iris hard, as if she'd been a piece of him that had been missing. "How's your head?" he asked. "You were hit with a pretty hard tranquilizer."

"Two darts," Iris said. "I'm good. The cold helped wake me up. When did you join the Jackals?"

Mack chuckled. A slight smile turned at the corner of his mouth and then his lips brushed hers.

"You'll never guess who I ran into wearing that camo-green Jackal's mask outside the mayor's door," he said. "Travis Otis, that rather nasty security guard who used to work for the mayor and had a history of domestic assault. You can't believe how surprised I was when I ripped his mask off and saw Travis's face."

Iris whistled. The vile man who'd been fired from the mayor's security detail after threatening Iris had gotten a new job as a Jackal.

"I'm certain he's the same man who shot me months ago and has been pursuing you," Mack said.

"You were right," she said, "you did know him."

"Well, I'm sorry to scare you," he said. "But I needed that confession on tape. I didn't want this case resting on just my word and yours. Not after everything that happened. She's too powerful to arrest without irrefutable evidence and I didn't want to put you in the position of being the only witness to a major crime again. You deserve to be free to live your life knowing the person who hurt you is put away for good. And we needed her confession to get other witnesses to come forward."

"Thanks for that," she said.

Yeah, it was nice to know that this time the weight of seeing justice done wouldn't all be on her shoulders.

"RCMP are on their way," he added. "Of course we're on the top floor of a triple-decker yacht with a whole bunch of security people with guns hanging around the lower level. I did my best to avoid them, but had to knock down and tie up a few, including Travis. It's only a matter of time before their buddies find them or us. My only goal was sneaking onto this boat, getting to you and getting off alive. I'm leaving the mass arrests up to the other cops."

She gazed at his face, wanting to memorize every curve and every line. She hoped she never lost sight of him again. "How did you find me?"

"Liam arrested me. Seth helped me figure out the red-masked Jackal and the people who pulled you into the helicopter were from the homeless center."

"They need help," Iris said quickly. "They were vulnerable and in need, and the mayor forced them into this." She knew how tempting the mayor's offer could be and where her own life could've been without God's grace and her family.

"I knew you'd say that," Mack said, and squeezed her tighter. "Jess and our friend Noah arrested the red-masked Jackal and the two who got you into the helicopter. Their real names are Joseph, Sara and Elliot by the way. They've all agreed to testify and also help find scholarship recipients who were forced into doing the mayor's dirty work. They also all hope you're okay and want you to know they're sorry."

Thank You, God.

"I can't wait to see them," Iris said. It didn't matter what they'd done. The important thing was who they chose to be now. "How did you find them?"

"The helicopter tipped me off they might be connected to wealth," Mack said. "Seth found their identities, and sure enough they were all from rich families, so I called my father for help—"

"Your father?" Her arms tightened around him. She couldn't imagine how hard it had been for Mack to overcome his pride like that.

"Yeah," Mack said. "I know I said I'd never ask him for help, but I couldn't risk losing you. My mom is hoping you'll come over for dinner, by the way. I can't promise there won't be a whole lot of family drama, but it will be my family and it will be real."

Something swelled in her heart as she realized what it meant that he was opening up his life to her.

"Dad remembered that all three of the young people were recipients of the mayor's scholarship programs," he went on. "Apparently it was a big deal around his country club. Seth tracked the mayor to her yacht. Liam's been coordinating with police. I came for you." He looked down at her. His hand brushed her face. "I'm always going to come for you."

"Well, I was planning on escaping and then rescuing you," she said.

He chuckled. "I'm not surprised." He pulled away, opened the door a crack and glanced out. She followed his gaze. The coast seemed clear.

"Your ride is here," Liam's voice came again. "Starboard side."

"Copy that," Mack said. "We're on our way."

His left hand slid into hers. With the other, he kept his weapon at the ready. They slipped out onto the empty deck and started running. Shouting voices and heavy footsteps rose in the distance. He reached a doorway and paused to make sure it was clear, and then they ran down a narrow spiraling staircase, until they reached the next deck. At the railing, they looked down. There far below them sat Liam at the wheel of a small rescue dinghy. Mack waved at him and then pulled a rope from somewhere inside his jacket and anchored it over the edge.

"You okay to climb?" Mack asked. She nodded, and he smiled. "I'll see you down there."

Iris took the hand he offered and climbed over the railing. Then she turned around and braced herself against the side of the boat, held the rope with one hand and Mack's strong arm with the other. Icy gray water lay beneath her. Freezing wind lashed her body. She let go of Mack and gripped the rope with both hands. "Thank you for coming for me."

"Always," he said. "See you down there."

The voices grew louder. Figures pelted around the corner. And then she saw him, like something out of a nightmare—Travis Otis was running toward them.

"Stop!" He raised his weapon. "Right now or I'll shoot!"

"Iris, go!" Mack shouted. "Don't stop! I've got this!"

Her heart caught in her throat as Mack spun toward the man, placing himself between her and danger. He raised his weapon. But it was too late. Travis had already fired. His bullet split the air, catching Mack hard in his chest.

Mack stumbled backward, his body struck the railing and he fell over the side.

Pain swept through Mack's body from the unexpected gut-punch of the bullet that had lodged in his bulletproof vest. As he fell, he could hear Iris screaming from above. Then he felt the cold, hard impact of the freezing water. He gasped and the choppy waves swept over him.

Help me, Lord. Please help me, Lord.

He struggled to take off his bulletproof vest and equipment weighing him down, battling against the numbing cold of the water. He hadn't remembered anything the first time he'd been shot and drowned. He'd just vaguely been aware of the sensation of numbness in his body, and then air moving rhythmically through his lungs and the softness of the bed beneath him as he slowly came back into consciousness. But this time he was painfully aware of the unrelenting power of the water sucking him down. Darkness filled his eyes. Pain engulfed his lungs.

Then a splash struck the water above him. A figure

swam toward him, and a hand reached for him, pulling him up toward the surface.

Mack broke through the water and felt the sting of winter wind on his face. Gunshots shook the air around them. He gasped as strong, gloved hands gripped his body, one at his collar and one at his back, and hauled him into a dinghy.

"Stay low!" It was Liam. "I managed to ping the shoulder of the guy who was shooting at you and he's fallen back. But it's only a matter of time before the gunfire attracts backup."

But if Liam was in the boat, who'd jumped in to rescue him?

Mack turned to see Iris's exhausted and smiling face as she clung to the side of the boat.

"Iris…" Mack panted.

Liam hauled her in, and she crawled over to Mack and collapsed on the bottom of the boat beside him. Mack wrapped both arms around her and held her against his chest.

Liam tossed an emergency blanket at them and then gunned the engine. Iris helped Mack pull the blanket over both of them and then she leaned against his chest.

"Just for the record," Liam said loudly over the wind, "I was going to jump in after you if you hadn't figured it out. But she dropped out of the sky from that rope like some kind of action movie star and dived in before I could stop her." He grinned. "And I would've tried. But she's pretty tenacious."

Yeah, she was. Mack looked down at Iris, as she lay there panting and shivering against him, letting their warmth fill and surround each other. She was tenacious and beautiful, kind and forgiving, stubborn and strong. She was everything he could've ever hoped for and far more than he'd ever hoped to find.

The sound of motors grew loud. Something was coming toward them. He pushed himself up on one arm and looked past Liam. A fleet of police helicopters and boats was approaching. Liam exchanged a few short words with someone on the other end of the radio, but his conversation was lost to the rush of the wind. Then Liam glanced back at them.

"Tell them the mayor's former chief of security, Travis Otis shot Mack," Iris said over the noise, "and that he's a Jackal."

"Will do," Liam said. "Looks like a total of six young people who were abducted by the Jackals ended up working for the mayor. Thanks to the confession Iris got out of Mayor Kats, they've all agreed to testify against her and help locate any others. Hearing the audio of the mayor ordering them killed really clinched it. Seth's also tracked down the offshore money transfer that the mayor used to pay Hank Barrie to kill Oscar Underwood and frame you, Mack. And now Barrie's flipped faster than a pancake. You're in the clear and the charges against you are being dropped as we speak. Investigators will be meeting Iris when we dock to get her statement."

He glanced down at his phone and then back to them.

"Mack, it's up to you if you want to stick around for the arrests," Liam said, "or if you want me to get you out of here before anyone realizes you were part of this operation. I don't know what cover story you're wanting to go with about everything that's happened, or who you want us to say was here, but the press is going to be all over this. It's going to make it harder for your next undercover assignment."

"There won't be any more undercover assignments," Mack said, tightening his arm around Iris. "At least not ones that force me to pretend to be someone else for days, let alone weeks or months at a time. I'm going to get a transfer out of undercover work and try living my own real life for a change."

Liam nodded slowly, then turned his back on them and snapped his phone to his ear. Whoever he was talking to and whatever he was saying was lost to the wind, the motors and the waves.

And that was okay with Mack. He'd regroup with his team soon enough. They were amazing and he trusted them with his life. For now, the only thing that mattered was the woman in his arms.

He looked down at Iris. She turned her face toward him and he gently cupped one hand to her cheek.

"You're letting other cops arrest the mayor and Travis," she said. "You're letting other people storm the boat and interrogate other Jackals. This is a huge arrest and you're not getting the credit."

"I don't need the credit or the spotlight," Mack said. "I just need you. Iris, I love you. I'm not sure when I first fell in love with you, maybe it's something that's been building since that very first moment we met. All I know is I kept falling deeper and deeper in love with you the more time we spent together. That's why I got so involved at the homeless center and stayed late so many nights, just helping you clean up and getting to know you. That's why I disregarded orders… I couldn't just stand back when the green-masked Jackal was stalking you. And that's why I fought so hard to find you when you went on the run."

Her lips parted but she didn't speak.

Mack's fingertips brushed the wet strands of hair that fell around her face. "I have been in love with you so long, Iris, I can't imagine life without you," he said. "I want to be the one who comes to find you whenever you need someone. I want to be the one who holds your hand, does the dishes with you and comes home to you every night for the rest of our lives."

Happiness shone in her eyes. "I love you, too."

He leaned forward and kissed her, without hesitation or doubt. Her hands reached around his neck and she kissed him back.

The sound of the fleet grew into a roar. He pulled away, cradling her into his side, and looked up. Helicopters and boats flew past them on all sides.

Liam turned back toward them. The twinkle in his eye made Mack pretty sure that Liam had spotted the kiss.

"Update," Liam said. "Warrants have been issued for the mayor and six members of her staff. Several police officers have come forward to say the mayor was putting pressure on them to downplay the accusation against Oscar Underwood and put you on probation. And the Gravenhurst Family Trust has publicly extended an offer of support to help Iris rebuild the homeless center."

"That will be my mother's doing," Mack murmured, pulling Iris closer. "Like I said, she wants to meet you. It's completely up to you whether you decide to accept their help. If not, there will be other people stepping up, I'm sure of it."

"Agreed." Liam nodded. "Several of us have contacts, big and small, who'll be happy to chip in. Also, Mack, rumor is that you're officially getting your badge back by tomorrow. Looks like it's finally all over."

Liam flashed them a grin and then turned back to his phone. Iris nestled deeper into Mack's arms. He bent down and brushed a kiss across her cheek.

"Will you marry me?" he whispered. "I'm not saying life with me will be easy. But I know for certain that I don't ever want to spend another day without you."

"I will absolutely marry you." A smile brushed her lips and illuminated her eyes. "It's you and me, forever."

As he leaned down and kissed her again, Mack knew without a doubt that the best story of his life was just beginning.

* * * * *

Dear Reader,

I was eleven years old when I decided to become an author, and thirteen when I started really trying to write books. I still have all of my early tries stashed away in my cupboard. My handwriting was so terrible, I crossed out so many things, and crammed so many words on a page that I can barely read them. But I can still smell the lingering fruits of the different scented pens I used to write with. It wasn't until I was twenty-four that I started writing the first full-length book I'd ever publish. (In fact, I started it on the road trip I mentioned on the dedication page.) I sold that book nine years later, when I was thirty-three.

The book you now hold in your hands is my twentieth.

I'm here because of hundreds of people, far more than I could ever count or list here. There are friends, readers, agents, editors, people who read my first tries and people who supported me. People who gave me space to write in their B and Bs, and coffee shops I worked in. Fellow writers who taught me how to write better. Countless members of law enforcement, the military and people I trained with at the dojo who helped me choreograph scenes.

And I want to thank you, my readers, for all of your encouragement. I can't tell you how many times I've been discouraged and received a note or message from you that has encouraged me to keep going. You have given me strength and hope when I'm feeling defeated, and I am eternally grateful for you.

Thank you for sharing this journey with me,
Maggie

SPECIAL EXCERPT FROM

LOVE INSPIRED SUSPENSE
INSPIRATIONAL ROMANCE

*Framed for her foster brother's murder,
FBI special agent Wren Santino must clear her
name—but someone's dead set on stopping her from
finding the truth. Now with help from her childhood
friend Titus Anderson, unraveling a conspiracy
may be the only way to survive.*

Read on for a sneak preview of
Falsely Accused *by Shirlee McCoy,*
available March 2020 from Love Inspired Suspense!

Titus turned onto the paved road that led to town. Wren had said Ryan was there. Ambushed by the men who'd been trying to kill her.

He glanced in his rearview mirror and saw a car coming up fast behind him. No headlights. Just white paint gleaming in the moonlight.

"What's wrong?" Wren asked, shifting to look out the back window. "That's them," she murmured, her voice cold with anger or fear.

"Good. Let's see if we can lead them to the police."

"They'll run us off the road before then."

Probably, but the closer they were to help when it happened, the better off they'd be. He sped around a curve in the road, the white car closing the gap between them. It tapped his bumper, knocking the Jeep sideways.

He straightened, steering the Jeep back onto the road, and tried to accelerate into the next curve as he was rear-ended again.

This time, the force of the impact sent him spinning out of control. The Jeep glanced off a guardrail, bounced back onto the road and then off it, tumbling down into a creek and landing nose down in the soft creek bed.

He didn't have time to think about damage, to ask if Wren was okay or to make another call to 911. He knew the men in the car were going to come for them.

Come for *Wren*.

And he was going to make certain they didn't get her.

Don't miss
Falsely Accused *by Shirlee McCoy,*
available March 2020 wherever
Love Inspired Suspense books and ebooks are sold.

LoveInspired.com

LISEXP0220

LOVE INSPIRED

INSPIRATIONAL ROMANCE

UPLIFTING STORIES OF FAITH, FORGIVENESS AND HOPE.

Join our social communities to connect with other readers who share your love!

Sign up for the Love Inspired newsletter at **LoveInspired.com** to be the first to find out about upcoming titles, special promotions and exclusive content.

CONNECT WITH US AT:

f Facebook.com/LoveInspiredBooks

🐦 Twitter.com/LoveInspiredBks

Facebook.com/groups/HarlequinConnection

HARLEQUIN

Heartfelt or suspenseful, inspiring or passionate, Harlequin has your happily-ever-after.

With new books published every month, you are sure to find the satisfying escape you know you deserve.

SIGN UP FOR THE HARLEQUIN NEWSLETTER

Be the first to hear about great new reads and exciting offers!

Harlequin.com/newsletters